Chapter One

The Secret

The first to speak was a big guy dressed in a checked shirt and baggy trousers held up by braces. He had the rugged appearance of someone who had been working outside all his life, with red cheeks above an unkempt beard. He introduced himself as John but people called him 'Big John', a nickname given to him at school.

Jackson's Farm was well known in the village. It was a well-established farm that had been run by the Jacksons for decades and Big John was the last of them. All his life his father had reminded him that the farm would be his one day. John could never bring himself to tell his father that, although he didn't mind the hard work, he didn't want the responsibility of running the farm. But it was taken for granted that the son would carry on the tradition of farming. That tradition dominated his life.

Big John had never married or had children. Since his parents had passed away, his only companion was his dog, Meg. And because he had no one to share his problems with, John tended to worry about most things; but his biggest worries were: the fear of anything happening to his animals, and not keeping up the payments on the large bank loan his father had taken out to modernise the farm.

He worked from dawn to dusk. It was the only way he knew to make the payments on the loan. He would only employ casual workers as a last resort, when he couldn't find enough hours in the day to get the work done.

John's highlight of the day was when the postman brought the mail. It was his way of catching up on the local news or gossip and having a five-minute break from work.

It was dark and it had been a long day. John came in through the door as usual and made his way to his old chair in front of the range. Meg sat down beside him and put her head on his knee for her routine stroke.

"Five minutes, Meg, and we're getting something to eat," he said to her.

She looked at him and made a little whine as if she understood. On the range was some stew he had cooked yesterday. He always made enough to last him several days and tonight all he had to do was dish it out.

Meg's bark at the door woke him up from his chair.

"What's up, girl?"

With her nose to the door, Meg started to bark again. Feeling a bit stiff from sleeping in the chair, John got up and went to the window. He drew the curtain to one side and looked out.

"There's nobody there, Meg. Go lay down."

John looked at the clock above the range and could see he had been asleep for some time as it was past midnight, but it wasn't unusual for him to do that.

"Well, Meg, I'm going up now. See you in the morning. Hold the fort."

Meg, who was lying down, raised her head to look at him as the light went out.

John was woken by the sound of a chair being knocked over downstairs. He knew it would not have been Meg, as she never moved from her mat in the night. Yet, if there was someone down there, Meg would have been barking long before anyone had come in. Very quietly, John picked up his father's old shotgun, which was always by the side of his bed, and slowly made his way down the stairs.

Immediately, his attention was drawn to a cold wind blowing in the room; he could see it was coming from the front door. It was slightly open. Instantly he knew something was wrong as he was positive he had closed and locked the door last night. Although the light in the room was dim, he could make out that Meg wasn't in her place in front of the range and a chair from the end of the table was over on its side. John went over to the door and opened it fully. He always kept a flashlight on the porch shelf and he felt for it. As the beam scanned the path, he could see Meg. She was lying on the path, completely still.

He quickly went over to her. She was breathing but did not respond to his touch or voice. Beside her he could see some meat that she had probably eaten and some more bits that trailed along the path, obviously to entice her away from the house. By the unusual smell of it, he could guess that it was either poisoned or laced with a strong sedative. As she was still breathing, he concluded it was the latter.

He knew something was terribly wrong and his mind was reeling. *Who opened the door and enticed Meg out? Were they still inside or had they gone?* There was only one way to find out.

Because there hadn't been anybody in the room he had just come through, he felt it safe to go back in. Tucking the gun under his arm, he picked Meg up and made his way inside. The next thing he knew was a crashing blow to the back of his head; all he could see was the floor rising up towards him.

When he opened his eyes, he was aware that Meg's soft body was under his head. Dropping her had saved him from being hurt even more than he already was as she had cushioned him from the stone floor. She was still unconscious and he hoped and prayed she hadn't been damaged by the fall. He didn't know how long he had been lying there, or even if whoever had hit him was still in the house. But then the noise of footsteps and drawers being opened upstairs confirmed his fears.

Unsteadily, he got to his feet. He touched the back of his head where it hurt so much and could feel wetness; and as he took his hand away he could see blood on it. However, he knew that was the least of his worries. *Where was his gun?* There was no sign of it in the room so whoever it was upstairs had it with him.

John's instincts told him to get out and get help but he could feel rage bubbling up inside him that someone had hit him and was now ransacking his house. He had felt the same rage before when an 1800 lb bull had charged him, knocking him to the ground. By the time John had finished, the bull knew who was the master. And now no mere man, however big, was going to get the better of him.

John quietly made his way up the stairs. From the top he could see that the door of the little box room was wide open, revealing that nobody was in there. A drawer falling to the ground told him the intruder was next door in his bedroom. The door was partially closed, which was good for John, as he needed to step past the door. As he peered through the gap, he could see the back of the man rummaging through his things. He could see that this guy was big - even taller and wider than him, but compared to the bull, a mere man. He was sure, even though the guy had his gun, that he could take him as he had the element of surprise on his side. As far as the intruder was concerned, John was lying unconscious downstairs.

John quickly stepped past the gap of the doorway and waited to one side. He knew that when the man came out he wouldn't be looking his way as there were no other rooms up there - so he would be heading for the stairs. With his back to the wall, John heard the door opening wider and, as he thought, the guy came out without seeing him. The man was carrying the gun in his left hand and had a bag in the other. John was sure that it would contain, among other things, his savings, which had been hidden under clothes in the drawer.

It was now or never! He had to make his move if the element of surprise was to work. John grabbed him by the shoulder from behind and swung him around so his face came into contact with John's right fist. The gun and bag fell to the ground and the big guy went crashing into the wall at the top of the stairs. Before he could recover, John followed it through by throwing himself at the intruder and hitting him hard again, splitting the guy's cheek to the bone.

But it wasn't hard enough. John felt a sledgehammer-like blow to his stomach, which took the wind out of him and doubled him up. He could see a knee coming up towards his face, but his quick reaction took his head to one side and he grabbed the leg as it made its way up. With all his strength and with both hands, he threw the leg upwards, forcing the man over backwards.

John could see him reaching for the gun, which was lying nearby. He knew that he had to get it first or it would be all over for him. As he made his move, he saw that the guy was now on his feet with the gun pointed at him. John grabbed the barrels with both hands and pushed them to one side as one of the barrels went off, making a splintered hole in the wooden panel wall. It was his strength against the bigger man's. He daren't let go of the barrels to try and hit him as they wrestled with the gun at the top of the stairs.

From out of nowhere, he felt a crashing blow to the bridge of his nose as the guy head-butted him. Dazed, he felt blood running from his nose into his mouth. He could see this guy had been a fighter, trained to use every part of his body. He knew he had to hang on to the gun and keep it as close to him as he could, but the head- butt had caused his grip to loosen and brought the barrels to a vertical position between them. John felt another blow to his forehead from a second head-butt, which made his head jolt backwards. The next thing he heard was a deafening bang from the other barrel. As though in slow motion, he saw the big guy go flying backwards down the stairs.

John stood with the gun in both hands looking at his assailant, lying in a twisted heap covered in blood at the bottom of the stairs. He was trying to figure out how the big guy was at the bottom of the stairs and he wasn't. He realised that the head-butt must have jolted the gun in the man's hands, somehow pulling the trigger and that the reason he himself wasn't hurt was that the head-butt had caused his own head to go backwards, away from the blast.

He made his way down to see if he was alive. By the hole in his chest and the way his neck was twisted from landing, he could see he was dead.

John went to the phone, picked up the handset and dialled, which was no easy task as his hands were shaking violently.

"Emergency. Which service do you require?" the voice said.

John was about to speak but found himself replacing the handset.

I need time to think, he said to himself, trying to clear his racing mind. He remembered an incident that he had seen on the News not long ago, where two men had broken into a farmhouse. The farmer had come downstairs with his shotgun and, as the two went for him, he shot at them, killing one and wounding the other. He called the police to report what had happened, thinking he was in the right in defending himself, but it ended up with **him** being imprisoned for the death.

Now he found himself in a similar situation! It wasn't too late to ring the police but, knowing what happened to the farmer, he couldn't take the chance of ending up in the same boat.   He told himself: *The chance of anybody knowing he was here would be remote; after all if you were going to break into a place, it's not something that you would go around telling everyone. And it's so remote here that nobody would have heard the gunshots. Besides, it's not as if I took a shot at him; his own action made the gun go off.*

All he had to do was bury the body somewhere on the farm and no one would be any wiser. It seemed like a good plan, that nothing could go wrong with, but he had to work fast under the cover of dark. He went to the barn, started up the digger and made his way to the open-sided Dutch barn where the hay was stored. He chose that place because it was furthest from the house, and no one would go there except him. He needed to remove a section of the hay bales and dig a pit.

It wasn't long before the pit had been dug. He made his way back to the house with the digger, and went inside, taking a plastic sheet with him. He laid out the sheet on the floor and dragged the body onto it then wrapped it up. Next, he made his way outdoors, rolled the body into the long bucket of the digger, and took it back to the barn. He unwrapped the body and rolled it into the pit.

As he did when he buried an animal, he covered it with lime to speed up the decomposing process, and continued to backfill the earth. When he had finished he compressed the loose earth with the bucket of the digger so that there wouldn't be any signs of disturbance. Having restacked the hay on top, he stood there for a while making sure nothing looked suspicious. It looked fine.

He put the digger away and went back into the house thinking that was it, but his eyes went to the pool of blood at the bottom of the stairs. He spent the rest of the night cleaning away every trace of blood and any evidence of an intruder. It was almost light and he had to be up as usual for the animals, and to meet the postman in case he came. He knew things had to appear normal. Mentally and physically exhausted, he slumped into his chair in front of the range. The last thing he saw was Meg, who was still in the position he had placed her.

John was woken by Meg putting her chin on his knee. Placing his hand on her head, he said, "Nice to see you back, Meg." She made a little whine. As if he knew what she was saying, he said, "Yes, Meg, that was something of a night."

It all came back to him. His mind started to question whether he had done the right thing. Should he have phoned the police? But even if there had been a chance of not being charged, it was too late now, as they would know that he had deliberately tried to cover up what had happened by burying the body. And, as true as it was that he hadn't shot the intruder, they wouldn't believe his story so he'd definitely be locked away for a long time. Now there was no going back.

As John got up, an intense pain shot through his head. He made his way over to the mirror and saw his nose was swollen and there was blackening around his eyes. He would have to come up with a cover story in case anyone called, such as Joe the postman. Fortunately he sometimes didn't call for a week and hopefully it wouldn't show by then but, in case, he made up a story - that he was head-butted by one of the cows, which could easily happen in reality so would be convincing.

Although John was always busy the haunting memory of that night interrupted his work as he often found himself lost in thought and worrying about what had happened. At night he kept reliving the fight at the top of the stairs and hearing the sound of the gun going off, then waking up in a cold sweat. He was hoping that, as it had been nearly a week, the memory of it would fade a little. But instead the memories intensified so much that he found himself in a series of nightmares, where he would open his eyes and see, standing at the bottom of his bed, the figure of the man - covered in blood with his head lying flopped to one side and half his chest missing. Then another time he would find himself standing in the Dutch barn looking at the place where he had buried the man, when the bales of hay would tumble from their stack, and suddenly an upright arm would force its way up through the earth, followed by a head and then body, clawing its way out of the grave and making its way towards him. He was scared to sleep and dreaded the nights.

Meg's barking woke him. Looking at his watch, he realised that, for the first time, he had overslept. Looking out of the window, he could see the postman's van outside the gate. John was already dressed, as lately he had been sleeping in his clothes on top of the bed. He rushed down to the gate.

"Morning, John."

John tried to keep his head down. He replied, "Morning, Joe."

As Joe handed him his mail, John forgot himself and raised his head to thank him.

Joe said, "What 'appened to you?"

John related the story of the cow to him.

"That looks painful. You could have been knocked out! You need to be careful, John. You being 'ere on your own – it don't bear thinking about. Anything could 'appen and nobody would know. Take care of yourself; I'll see you soon." As he was about to get into the van he stopped and said, "Did you 'ear about that escaped prisoner from up the road? The police are going 'ouse to 'ouse, asking if anyone seen 'im."

"How long ago was that?" John asked.

"About five days ago. Maybe a week."

"No, I haven't seen or heard anything about it."

"You need to keep your eyes open, John, especially being 'ere on your own."

"I can take care of myself, Joe, and besides nobody ever comes here, but will do," John assured him.

John knew from what Joe said that it wouldn't be long before he had a visit from the police but, if he kept calm and didn't say too much, they wouldn't suspect anything.

It had been a few days since he last saw Joe and he was up on the barn roof making repairs. He could hear Meg barking.

"Okay, Meg, it's only the postman."

John climbed down and went to the gate. Sure enough it was Joe.

"Morning, Joe."

"Good morning, John."

But the conversation was far from good, as John was about to find out. It was a meeting that he would never forget.

11

"There's news of a suspected foot and mouth outbreak at Gideon's Farm," announced Joe.

"How long ago was that?"

"Yesterday afternoon, apparently. I 'ear they're talking of a meeting at the hall to discuss it this evening. You should be there, John."

One of John's biggest fears had come knocking at his door. The only thing that could be worse was that the police had come, suspecting that a body was buried on the farm! He remembered that, when he was a lad, his father had had to deal with an outbreak that almost ruined the farm, and that it had taken years to recover from. In fact, his father had only managed to come back from it because he didn't have the large debt to pay that John had. He knew now it was only a matter of time before the men from the Ministry would come to destroy his animals and close his farm as before. And all the talking in the world wouldn't stop it.

"There's no point, Joe. I'm sure if there's anything to hear you'll let me know."

"Of course I will but I still think you should go," replied Joe shaking his head.

All sorts of things were racing through John's mind. *Why me? Is this God's way of punishing me for hiding the death of that thief?*

"It may not 'appen," said Joe, trying to cheer him up.

"Not happen? I wish I could share your optimism!" replied John.

"Even if it did spread, John, you might be lucky. It might miss you."

But John knew otherwise. He knew how quickly the contagious disease could spread, especially as Gideon's Farm was only a quarter of a mile away and, under favourable weather conditions, the airborne virus could easily spread. And, even if it didn't come that way, it could be spread by people or even vehicles that had been contaminated by the virus.

Every day he would check the animals for signs and each day his worry increased. Then came the day when he thought some of the cattle were drooling more than usual – the long, syrupy strings and froth a tell-tale sign. Sure enough, his routine inspection revealed the symptoms of the dreaded disease. He could see blisters in the mouths and on the feet, which made the animals so lame that they couldn't walk. What he most feared had come upon him. Foot and mouth had arrived.

As hard as it was, and with tears in his eyes, he knew what he had to do. The last thing he wanted was to have people running all over his farm, but he knew he didn't have a choice. Within the first day of informing the authorities, the men from the ministry were occupying the farm and confirming what John already knew.

There was now a new sign on the gate next to 'Jackson's Farm':
'QUARANTINE'!

Big John's life was crumbling away before him. His sleep was fitful. He couldn't worry anymore about his animals - they had all gone. The mass slaughter had been heartbreaking and he had watched helplessly as the carcasses were burned, the stench lingering in his nostrils for days. But now other concerns were pressing in on him. As a large part of the farm's income came from the animals, and that had now stopped, he was getting behind with the payments on the massive loan.

John awoke to hear Meg barking. Looking out of the window he could see the postman's van driving off. Because he knew it could only be more bad news, he was reluctant to collect the mail at the gate, but decided to go, as not knowing would be worse.

He sat at the table, just staring at the envelope. It seemed like hours had gone by. He could tell it was from the bank as it was the same type of envelope as those that he had received over the last few months. Opening it at last, his fears were confirmed. The bank was foreclosing on the loan. Compensation from the government would arrive too late to save the farm. It was taking so long to be sorted out that many farmers were losing hope.

Up until that moment, he had been tempted to open the bottle of whisky that had been staring at him from the shelf, and had managed to resist it. But the news from the bank made him give in and seek relief from the despair that was pushing him into a dark and bottomless pit.

It wasn't long before John's home and farm were sold, leaving him penniless. His emotions were divided: sadness for the loss of the home that had been in his family for generations and for letting his father down; yet, now he had come to terms with it, there was a sense of release from the millstone of worry that the farm had been to him all these years.

All that Big John had left was his father's shotgun - which he couldn't part with, even though it brought back terrible memories, and the half-full bottle of whisky that had been his comfort over the last week. And of course, Meg, who followed him wherever he went.

He closed the farm gate for the last time and made his way off. The folk on the neighbouring farm had offered to let him stay there and, not knowing where he would go, he decided to take them up on their offer.

John was a very proud person and didn't want anyone feeling sorry for him, and the kindness of the people there was too much for him. The conversation around the meal table was about how his father's father had started the farm and that if his father was alive he might have saved it. That made him feel worse and he just wanted to be alone with his thoughts. He tormented himself, worrying that whoever bought the place might just uncover the remains of the body, but he couldn't stay either. He knew he had to try and get as far away as possible. So he decided to tell the people that it was time to move on.

"Where will you go, John?" they asked.

"Not sure, but I need to put all this behind me."

"We understand, John. Remember, if wherever you end up doesn't work out, you always have a place here."

"Thanks. There is just one thing, if I can ask you. Can I leave Meg here with you? I don't think it would be fair on her, taking her away."

"Sure, John, you know we will take good care of her."

When John opened the door Meg got up to follow. "Stay Meg!" he said and closed the door. With a little whine Meg sat with her eyes fixed on the door.

Where he was going he didn't know, but he knew he couldn't have taken Meg with him. One thing he did know was that it would be a life free from worry, however it turned out.

A day of walking took him into territory that he had never been to before. He found himself wandering down a country lane and, as the light was fading and fog seemed to be settling in, he knew he would have to find somewhere to rest for the night. He could see up ahead was a wooded area. Not knowing where the nearest town or village was and being a countryman, he decided to find a place in the woods, especially as now there seemed to be a storm blowing up and it had started to rain hard.

As he approached the entrance to the woods, looking to take shelter under a tree, he could hear the sobs of a child, which made him look around. There standing a little way off the track into the woods was a young girl.

He couldn't help noticing the colour of her skin. It looked as if it had never seen the sun. It was so white that it made her dark, almost black, eyes appear piercing as she looked at him, and the contrast with her long, black hair was quite startling. Nevertheless, here was an innocent child that needed help.

John made his way over and said, "What's up, little one?"

"I've lost my daddy. I can't find him."

"Where did you lose your daddy?"

"Somewhere in the woods. I ran off a little way to chase a rabbit. Daddy told me not to go far or I might get lost, and now I can't find him."

Trying to comfort her, he asked, "What do they call you?"

"Daddy calls me his special Little Angel."

"Okay then, Little Angel, that's what I'll call you."

"Will you come and help me find my daddy?"

John knew it wasn't a situation he should be letting himself get into, a stranger alone with a young child, but what choice did he have? How could he resist the cry of help from a little girl pulling on his heartstrings?

Hoping there was a chance of someone being nearby, he went back to the lane to see, but there was nobody around. As every fibre inside him was saying *don't go into the woods with her*, he felt the hand of the little girl take hold of his, pulling him into the woods, saying, "Please come! Daddy's not far away. Please, please, help me find him!"

"We had better stay on the track, Angel. We don't want us getting lost."

"Daddy is over there - in that direction," she announced as she pointed into the trees.

"How do you know it's this way?"

She didn't answer his question but said, "It's not much further," pulling his hand harder as she led the way.

Before he knew it, Angel had led him off the track and deeper into the woods.

John wanted to say to her: "For someone lost, how come you seem to know the trails of the woods?" But, as she was only a little child and it might have upset her further, he couldn't bring himself to say that to her. But the question lingered.

He came to a halt. Up ahead, in the direction Angel was taking him, was a wall of dense fog, deep in the wood.

"Angel, we must go back! If we enter into that fog we will both be lost."

With both her hands now tightly gripping John's hand, and as if she had supernatural strength, she pulled John along towards the fog.

"I know Daddy is just up ahead! Please, please - we have to find him!"

Just at that moment a crack of thunder echoed across the treetops and caused the nesting crows to fill the woods with the sound of their cawing.

Not being sure if it was the sound of the crows or the sound of the thunder distorting what he heard, John could have sworn the word 'him' from the little girl, sounded like the husky voice of an old man as they entered the fog.

A sudden chill went through his body, followed by intense pain in the hand that Angel was holding. Looking down to see why his hand was hurting so much, he pulled back in horror. He could see it was no longer the hand of a sweet, innocent child holding his, but something from the pit of Hell, a scaly creature with lifeless black eyes that seemed to pierce his soul as he gazed into them. His natural reaction made him try to pull his hand away, but the long twisted nails of the creature's claw tore into John's hand, ripping his flesh away as it held him tight, resisting what little strength he could muster.

With a growling, unrecognisable voice, and breath that stank with the putrid smell of rotten flesh, it said, "Mine! Mine!" as if it was taking prey back to its lair.

Desperate fear and the excruciating pain in his hand gave John the extra strength he needed to pull his hand away and run for his life.

He had lost all sense of direction, and in a panic-stricken state, instead of running to safety back the way he had come, he ran further into the dense fog. John knew he had to keep going for he knew that, not far behind him, was a demon from Hell.

He had been running for what seemed like hours then stopped to rest with his back to a tree. After gaining a few breaths, he peered around the tree, hoping that he had lost the creature, but to his dismay, he could see it coming his way!

The air was becoming acrid with the smell from the creature. It started to make him retch and his eyes began to water, as it made its way closer to where he was. Feeling utterly helpless, John knew if he didn't think of something quickly he would be doomed.

He thought: *If I could figure out how to double back and get behind it, I might be in for a chance, or if I could somehow make it to the track, I could maybe make it out of the woods.*

The creature stopped yards away from him, sniffing the air to give it direction as to where he was.

John knew that if he was to make a move it had to be now. But as he started, to his horror, the crows in the trees above him started to caw. Instantly the demon's head turned towards him.

John ran as fast as he could to get some distance between him and the demon. He headed towards the direction he thought the track might be. He knew he had to make it, knowing that it was his only hope of escaping from what was coming after him, and a fate too fearful to even think about . . .

There wasn't an ounce of energy left in his body. It was crying out for rest, but he had to keep going. He didn't know how much more his body could take but he knew he had to rest somewhere that he wouldn't be found by the creature. He decided the safer option was to hide deeper in the woods rather than try to find the track.

After a while, unable to go any further, he found himself in front of a charred black tree that stood on its own, surrounded by a few fallen ones. He collapsed to the ground with his back to it and closed his eyes. The only thing that could be heard was John's heart pounding fast as his lungs were gasping for air. The intense burning pain in his hand and the cold dampness of the air brought him out of his short rest.

Opening his eyes and looking down at his hand, he could see that it was swollen and oozing with greenish yellow puss from the gouges of the creature's nails.

John knew about cuts from working with animals and how quickly they could become infected if unattended to. He had to do something quickly before the poison got into his veins. Taking the bottle of whisky from his pocket, he poured some over his hand and wrapped his hanky around it, but he could feel already the poison was taking effect on him. He started to shiver in the cold, damp atmosphere so he turned his collar up to keep in the little body warmth he had, and continued to sit there. He could feel his strength draining away as he tried to stay awake.

As he drifted in and out of sleep, an overwhelming sense of heaviness and guilt came upon him. It wasn't long before his mind started dredging up what he had done at the farm - secretly burying someone; then telling him again that he had let his father down and was a failure. Having experienced those same thoughts at the farm, he knew it was time for his comforter; feeling for the whisky bottle, he took a large swig to stop the depressing thoughts. All it did was cloud his mind and make him drowsier. With his eyes heavy and fighting to keep them open, his mind conjured up a picture of his farm neighbours pointing their fingers at him and raising their voices, accusing him of losing his father's farm.

A depressing voice entered his head, saying, "It was his fault. He is finished!" Unable to open his eyes, he heard several audible voices all around him, that seemed to come from within the tree he was leaning against, calling out, "Failure! Failure! Your life isn't worth living! You will always have worry!" If that wasn't enough, the face of the guy he buried appeared covered in blood, saying "Killer! Killer!"

John raised the bottle to his lips with the little strength he had left and finished off the whisky. Without realising it had happened, he found that his father's shotgun was out of its case.

The voices were intensifying, shrieking at him to end it all and saying, "Do it, Failure! Do it! Killer!" All he had to do was to look down the barrels and pull the trigger, and he would be free from it all. *One more swig of whisky should give me the courage*, he thought, but all that remained were a few drops that wet his lips.

He could feel the pressure intensifying on the trigger from his finger, and drops of sweat from his brow were running down his eyelids on to the barrels of the gun. The hostile voices all around him were chanting viciously at him to do it. Was it the drink, or was it the poison, or maybe both, in his system causing him to hallucinate? He was far from caring - he just wanted it all to stop.

Suddenly he heard a soft voice, that seemed to come from alongside, speaking into his ear: "John! Life may seem dark right now, but that can all change for you. Put the gun down."

Then in his other ear he heard, "Don't listen to him! We can help you."

"John, my words are life to you. Put the gun down."

"They're lies! Pull the trigger and all your cares will be over!" the voices urged.

John tried with all his might to open his eyes to see what was going on around him and who it was that had the soft voice, but all he could do was listen helplessly.

"That's enough, you two! He's spoken for. Now go!"

"We were here first. He's ours! He's no good to you; he's weak and ready to go with us. All he has to do is pull the trigger," the voices said in unison.

Raising his staff at them, the other being commanded, "Go back to the depths of despair from where you have come!"

"Nooooo! Never! We can't go back without him!"
With the power coming from the staff, they evaporated back into the tree.

John could feel the gun, as though it had a mind of its own, lower itself to the ground. Sitting there, unable to see and feeling completely vulnerable, he could sense someone was nearby. Without warning he felt a hand placed on his forehead, which made him raise his head from its slumped position. He could feel the heaviness of his eyelids disappearing and he was able to open his eyes. He turned his head to see the figure of a man in a robe sitting alongside him. John noticed his long hair and beard and the gnarled wooden staff in his hand.

With a weakened voice, he said. "Who are you? How did you get here?"

"My friends call me 'Jerry'. I think you could do with a friend right now, John."

John managed to say tiredly, "Yes, I haven't had many of those in my life, Jerry." Closing his eyes again, he was convinced he was having a conversation with nobody but himself. Then he heard:

"John, you will be okay now. I'm here to help you."

As he opened his eyes, he said, "Help me . . ." Unable to finish his words, he heard a distant bell ringing. Straining to see, he became aware that the old man was now standing in front of him with an aura of warm radiant light around him.

The fog and darkness of the wood seemed to know the authority of the light, and were giving way to it, receding back into the trees. He could feel that the influence of the whisky and the fever of the poison within him were leaving.

He just sat there as, even though he could feel a little strength returning, he was still too weak to move. He waited apprehensively for whatever was to happen next. "Big John Jackson, your life was not supposed to be filled with worry. Your cry for help has been heard and your anguish has been seen. I have been sent to help you, so that you can be free from your worries and burdens. I can show you the way to find hope and a bright future. It's your choice, John. Until you say, 'yes' to me, I am unable to help you."

He sat there, staring at Jerry, not saying anything at first. Then, out of desperation, he heard himself say, "Help me!"

Before he could say anything else, he found himself up on his feet, taking Jerry's outstretched hand. Confused, his mind filled with questions:

How does he know my name and what my life has been like? Does he know what I did? Had he been that drunk on whisky that all this was due to its effects?

"It's going to be alright. Come with me."

John had never had anyone to help him, or take control of any situation in his life. He felt himself giving in and found he was experiencing something that was

23

new to him: Relaxation. As they walked he felt that all his cares and worries had been left behind at the fallen tree and an overwhelming feeling of peace came upon him, for the first time since he could remember.

"I don't understand what's going on. Are you real?" John asked, for Jerry's words sounded distant, as in a dream. He could feel himself falling to the floor.

"I've got you, John," Jerry said as he supported him with his arm. "Not far now, just a little further."

John could feel a new strength going through him.

"We're here, John!"

John found himself standing at the doorway of an inn. He could hear the sound of singing and laughter coming from within.

"Go on in, John. It's a safe place."

John turned to look at Jerry who was walking back into the darkness of the woods. He called to him, "How do you know my name?"

"Don't concern yourself with that now, John. All will be revealed later," came the reply, fading into the distance.

Big John stood there for a moment, unsure if this was real or a dream or even the whisky. The last thing he could remember was sitting among the trees looking down the barrels of his father's shotgun. And then a scary thought entered his mind.

Maybe I pulled the trigger and this is what the afterlife is like. And the inn door is a gateway to another unknown journey.

But his reasoning was telling him that couldn't be, as he was hearing the sound of very real singing and laughter from the other side of the door. Remembering what had happened to his hand, he looked down to see that there wasn't even a mark on it!

Opening the door slowly, he made his way inside. The last time he had stepped foot inside a pub was on a rare occasion in his teens and that was many years ago.

He noticed a white-bearded old man behind the bar smiling at him, who said, "Come on in, John!"

John made his way over to the bar to ask him, "Could you tell me where I am?"

The old man replied, "We've been waiting for you, Big John. Your table is ready."

John had a thousand things on his mind. He stared at the old man thinking:

What's with all the long white beards around here? I'm sure this is the same guy as in the woods – or, if it isn't, it was his twin brother that was talking to me.

But he dismissed the thought as he had now convinced himself that it was all in his imagination.

"Sorry?" John said, not sure if he heard the old man correctly.

The latter just smiled and escorted John to the table where there was a glass of orange juice ready for him, which is what he normally drank - he didn't even like whisky. John just sat mesmerised, responding mechanically to people that were saying hello. Although he was alone at the table, and still confused, he was experiencing something that he had not known in a long time – company. He didn't feel so alone, and also, unusually, he still couldn't feel any worry. He found it was now replaced with a wonderful sense of freedom from deep down within his spirit.

Sitting there he didn't know what was going to happen next, but was content to receive whatever it was .

Chapter Two

Abandoned

The next person to tell her story was Esther Thompson. She was only eighteen but her clothes and heavy rimmed glasses made her look a lot older. She explained that she was brought up in an orphanage. She was found at the entrance in a wooden fruit box with a note saying, "Not wanted." A staff member found her as she arrived for work. The orphanage staff named her 'Ruth Harbour': 'Ruth' after the person who found her and 'Harbour' after the name of the orphanage. Its full name was 'Happy Harbour'.

Because Ruth never knew her parents, or ever found out why she was abandoned, she felt rejected and alone, and certainly not happy, as some of the staff had nicknamed her.

The only person who showed her any real affection was the staff member who found her. Ruth called her 'Aunty Ruth'. Whenever Aunty Ruth had time, she would read her stories from the Bible. Ruth's favourite was the story of her namesake, Ruth. Aunty Ruth would tell her that she was special, because she had the same name as Ruth in the Bible. She repeated this to the other children, which resulted in them being cruel - not speaking to her, and calling her names. Staff members were not allowed to become attached to the children and, as Aunty Ruth obviously showed affection to her, she was transferred to another home.

Ruth became withdrawn and spent many years being rejected by prospective foster parents and had little hope of someone adopting her. If she did get close to any new friends, she knew they would soon be separated from her as they were found homes. She soon learned not to allow herself to become close to anyone. The only little friend that she could trust never to leave her was the rag doll that Aunty Ruth had given her before she was transferred.

She didn't even like the name she had been given. It always reminded her of her childhood and growing up feeling lost and abandoned. And then sometimes she had experienced dreams where she would hear a voice calling, "Esther! Esther!" Puzzled, she had asked Aunty Ruth who 'Esther' was and told her about the dreams. Aunty Ruth didn't seem to know, but her face looked quite concerned.

At the age of eighteen she was told that it was time for her to leave the orphanage and make her own way in life. Leaving with a few clothes and some books, she made her way to the nearby village.

The orphanage had arranged a room for her, and had paid the first month's rent. Although it was only a room, Ruth felt at home there; for the first time in her life she had something that was hers, and didn't have to share it with anyone else like she had to in the dormitory with all the other girls.

At first she found it hard to venture outside the room, but knew she had to try and make a little money to pay for the rent before the first month's payment had run out.

Ruth hadn't learnt any trade at the orphanage, as she found it hard to concentrate and was too withdrawn to ask for help. She soon found a way of making a living from selling flowers, but the money she made was hardly enough for food, let alone for the rent.

Some people bought her flowers because they were so full of colour and fragrance, but many because they felt sorry for her. Ruth didn't notice their colour. Growing up in the orphanage, she'd got used to the colour of the uniform, which was grey, and her self-esteem was so low that the clothes she wore were still grey. To Ruth, life was grey.

With her newfound love of exploring places, she would often go out in the evening to walk in the lanes that surrounded the village. Somehow she drew a kind of comfort from the stillness. Her closest companions were Loneliness and Depression. On her walks she would often talk to herself and sometimes pray and ask God why she had such a lonely life and, if possible, could he send her a friend.

It wasn't long before the rent was due as the month had soon passed. She knew that, with no money, she would have to leave her room and find somewhere else. Where she would go she had no idea.

If I could find Aunty Ruth I know she would take me in, she thought.

All Ruth knew was that she lived somewhere nearby in a village. But there were several villages, all in different directions. The only clue Ruth had about where she lived was from the times Aunty Ruth would tell her all about her little cottage: that she lived there with her cat, and that there was a stream running through the garden with a little wooden bridge over it, which she would cross to take a treat out for the horse in the field at the bottom of the garden. Ruth held that picture in her mind for years and always wished that she could visit and feed the horse.

Faced with four directions to choose from, she left it to chance. With her shabby little case of belongings, she made her way along one of the lanes. The first part of the lane she was familiar with, as she had been that far before. Although the sun was shining and the birds were singing, the uncertainty about where she would spend the night spoiled the day and started to bring on depressing thoughts. She therefore hadn't realised that she had walked further than before and found herself at the start of a winding track that led through the woods. Something stopped her from walking on although she didn't know why.

Boom! The heavens opened with a crack of thunder and the sound of crows cawing in the treetops filled the woods, ending her hesitation. She ran for cover into the woods to shelter under the trees.

She looked down the track and a chill ran down her spine as she heard a sound. She didn't know if it was her imagination, or the call of an animal, but it sounded very much like her name being called from out of the darkness of the woods. She soon dismissed it, but when she clearly heard her name being called again, another shiver went through her body. Someone or something was calling her into the woods. Half of her wanted to turn around and go back to the safety of her little room but she knew that she couldn't. She had nowhere to go now that she didn't live there anymore.

Something inside was telling her to run, but something stronger was urging her to take the first step into the woods, where the canopy was so dense it shut out most of the rain but a lot of the light as well.

"Ru-u-th, . . . Ru-u-th!" She heard her name being called once more.

She tried with all her strength to resist being drawn along the path, but something was taking over her will to resist.

She soon found herself deep in the woods. Suddenly the voices stopped. *Had they brought her to the place where they wanted her to be?* Appearing from the darkness of the trees was an elderly lady coming towards her. Her face looked familiar. *Aunty Ruth would be quite old by now. Could this be her?*

Feeling unsure, Ruth called out, "Aunty Ruth, is that you?"

"Yes, Ruth."

"What are you doing here? I've been trying to find you."

Reaching out to take Ruth's hand, she said, "I often come here. Come with me, Ruth. I will show you my special place."

Ruth, excited at seeing her again, took her hand. It felt icy cold!

"Why are you so cold, Aunty Ruth?"

She didn't reply but led Ruth further into the woods.

Ruth sensed that there was something strange about her as the Aunty Ruth she remembered would have been smiling and always talking, but this Aunty Ruth was not like that at all. However, the joy of seeing her again made Ruth put the thoughts to one side and she went with her.

They came to a small clearing where, surrounded by dead timbers, was a huge burnt tree.

"This is what I wanted to show you, Ruth, my favourite tree," said Aunty Ruth. "Go and sit on one of those logs. I won't be long."

Ruth watched her go off into the woods and couldn't help noticing that she left a trail of icy footprints in the dead undergrowth as she walked.

Looking around, waiting for Aunty Ruth to come back, she sat there in the quietness and darkness of the wood, trying to think of an explanation for the footprints of ice. She could feel an ominous atmosphere; the air was chilling and mist had started to swirl around her feet. The scene reminded her of a story from her favourite book, of a magical land and fairies, that Aunty Ruth would read to her. But this scene was far from a fairy book. If she had known what was going to happen, she would have made her way out of there fast.

It wasn't long before she heard her name again. This time it came in whispers:

"Ruth! . . . Ruth!"

Thinking it was Aunty Ruth, she started to look around but, to her disappointment, she was still on her own.

"Ruth, . . . Ruth!" she heard again. It was her two old companions, Loneliness and Depression, and they were trying to take advantage of the inhospitable place she had found herself in, reminding her of the dismal life she had.

In desperation she tried singing to blot out the depressing thoughts but, as she had never learnt any cheerful songs, it didn't work, so she started to pray her usual prayer to God about finding a friend. The more she prayed, the more her two companions were filling her mind with depressing words and chanting:

"You will *never* have a friend! No one wants to know you. You were meant to be alone in life. You will die lonely in the end!"

She had heard those words so many times that she was coming to believe that they were true. The voices intensified so much that she shut her eyes and covered her ears with her hands.

Opening her eyes she couldn't believe what lay before her. The mist was now a dense fog that surrounded her. She could only blame herself for not being able to resist entering the woods and, even if she could find her way back out to the lane, she would be stepping again into the unknown - where anything could happen, especially walking alone in the darkness and fog.

Oh, but then she decided that maybe the darkness of the lane would be safer than where she was. Just as she stood up, a crow landed in front of her and then another and before long there was a circle of crows around her. As she moved forward the crows moved closer, menacing her with their sharp beaks and making a squawking noise, forcing her back to where she had been sitting. She realised that they were not going to let her leave the woods.

Scared and not knowing how to get past the crows, she could see a small, distorted light in the distance from within the fog. It was coming towards her.

She held her breath, wondering if it might be someone carrying a torch. She would now welcome whoever owned the light if they could help her out of this situation.

At the orphanage the other children had been cruel to her, knowing how scared she was. They would play tricks on her and tell her scary stories of the creature who lived under her bed, that would wait till she was asleep and then take her away. One morning when she awoke she found her rag doll had gone. The others told her that the creature had taken it. Cuddling her rag doll at night had been her only means of keeping fear away but she never saw her doll again. After that she dreaded the nights, thinking she would be taken next.

There was something different about this light; it seemed to pulsate with a warm glow that lit up the canopy of trees. The nearer the light came, the brighter it shone, and the brightness made it hard for her to see. As she stood up, the crows flew off back into the treetops. Mesmerised by the light, she heard from out of the fog, the voice of Aunty Ruth, calling: "Run, Ruth! The light is evil. Keep away from the light. Run!"

She began to panic. Should she obey Aunty Ruth? Was the light really evil? After all, she reasoned, Aunty Ruth was the only person she could trust. But then she realised: *this wasn't the Aunty Ruth she knew!*

Before long, the light was in front of Ruth. The fog instantly went, then from out of the light came a gentle voice, "Esther, Esther Thomson, don't be afraid. I am here to help you. You don't have to be lonely anymore. Trust in the light and trust in me. The darkness brings only death. The choice is yours to make."

Instantly she recognised the voice. It was the one that been calling her in the night. It was reassuring, unlike the voice of 'Aunty Ruth'. So much so, that she found herself wanting to say: "Yes!" She spoke the word out with relief and the fear and the depressing voices of her two companions left her.

"Come, Esther, with me, I'll will take you to a place of safety."

Ruth did not know where the voice was leading her, but she didn't feel afraid. Anywhere was better than the wood and also it was the first time in her life that she felt safe and wanted, apart from when she was with the real Aunty Ruth.

As she proceeded down the lane, Ruth said boldly, "Sir, why do you keep calling me 'Esther Thompson'? I think you've made a mistake. My name is Ruth Harbour."

The voice replied, "That name doesn't belong to you. I named you Esther Thompson before you were born."

Not understanding, she asked. "Are you my father then?"

"You're not wrong in asking that, Esther. Yes, I am. You are a part of a big family and you have many brothers and sisters that love you as I do."

Excitedly she said, "Sir, what's your name?"

All her life she had longed to know who her father and mother were, and now, had she found her father?

"You can call me Friend," he said, then directed her to stop outside an inn. "We are here, Esther. As I promised, this is where you will find what has been missing in your life."

Before she could collect her thoughts enough to speak, the light disappeared into the darkness of the lane. She was confused and had so many questions she wanted to ask! If he was her father, as he said he was, why didn't he show himself? How had he found her? And why had he left her alone again outside an inn? She didn't understand. After all she had been through, had she been abandoned once again by her father?

There she was in the middle of nowhere, at a place she didn't know, nor would ever have gone to. She found herself walking through the inn door, to be confronted by a world she had never seen before. People's clothes seemed to be bright with rich, exaggerated colour; it was as if her eyes were now seeing things differently. Laughter and singing filled the air and, before she knew what was happening, people were coming up to her and asking her name. With newfound confidence, she heard herself say, "Esther Thompson."

The minute she said her name, it was as though her past had gone and she had a new beginning. Many people wanted to speak to her, but she couldn't help noticing the old, white-bearded man behind the bar smiling at her, beckoning her over to him.

"Esther," he said, "Welcome! We have been expecting you. There is someone I would like you to meet."

Without any hesitation, Esther replied, "You know me?"

The old man didn't answer. He just smiled and, taking her hand, took her over to the table where John was.

"John, this is Esther," he said. "Like you, John, she was lost, but now she has been found. I will leave her with you. You will have a lot in common to talk about."

With a smile on his face, the old man left them to get to know each other.

Assuming that John was a regular in the place, Esther took the lead in asking   questions. She wanted to know where this place was, and how it was possible that the old man knew her name, but she stopped short of telling him about what had happened in the woods and how she got to the inn. It was just too far-fetched, and if she told him, he would think she was some kind of weirdo.

"Esther is it? The truth? Like you, I don't know. I'm still asking myself the same questions."

Esther instantly warmed to him as she felt they indeed had something in common.

Chapter Three

Fate

Simon Peters was the next to tell his story. His tweed coat and glasses gave him the appearance of a well-educated man. By way of introduction, he said that he taught philosophy at the city university, and he was a great believer in fate. It was fate that had brought back into his life his long-lost childhood sweetheart, Mary. Mary and Simon, as children, had lived next door to each other. They would play together and were inseparable.

Once into their teen years, most of their friends were dating. But to Simon and Mary, dating wasn't anything new. It was so natural for them to be together.

Fate, however, had in store for them something else. Mary's parents were moving away and Mary had to go with them. Simon had never forgotten the day they parted. He was haunted by the pain in Mary's eyes as he had watched the car leave the street. Her tearful face looking out the back window had torn at his heart.

They had promised that they would write to each other every day. Simon waited each day before he left home for the post to arrive but there was no letter from Mary.

He spent his time imagining all sorts of reasons he hadn't heard from her. He couldn't even phone her as he was waiting for Mary to write him the number when they had the phone connected. He couldn't do anything but wait for the morning post.

Weeks turned into months and months into years, and he never knew what had happened to Mary or even where she was; or the reason why she had never written, but he could never forget the love of his life.

As the years passed Simon graduated, eventually becoming a lecturer and was offered a job working at a university in the north. He didn't really want to move in case Mary came back looking for him but time had diminished his hope and he resigned himself to whatever fate had in store for him.

His new job was lecturing on the subject of philosophy and he was ready for his first session. The lecture theatre was full and all eyes were fixed on him. Yet, as he was speaking, he couldn't help noticing the steady gaze of a young woman who looked achingly familiar. He was speaking and yet he couldn't hear his own voice. The woman's eyes had taken him back to the eyes full of sadness, saying goodbye from the rear car window. Applause from the students brought him back to the present. When he looked up from his notes he noticed that the woman had gone.

That night as he lay in bed he couldn't stop thinking about what had happened in the lecture room. Those eyes were so much like his Mary's. He fell asleep hoping that somehow she would be there at tomorrow's lecture.

The next day he got there extra early. The room began to fill up but there was no sign of the young lady. Simon found it hard to concentrate as he was continually looking around the room. To his disappointment the session finished without an appearance from her.

Everyone had left and Simon was packing his material away, when he heard, "Simon." He instantly knew the sound of that voice. He thought for a moment that it was a return of the flashbacks that he had had in the early days of losing Mary.

"Simon." He heard it again. He slowly turned around and there before him was Mary.

He stood there speechless. He had come to believe this moment would never happen. Mary held back nervously, not sure what Simon was thinking and fearing cold rejection. He saw her hesitation and held out his hand.

The next thing he knew they were embracing. For this moment the questions could wait. All they knew was that they had found each other again. Fate had separated them, and fate had brought them back together.

They clung to each other in overwhelming joy until he slowly eased her away from him. Keeping his hands on her shoulders, he asked hoarsely: "Why didn't you write?"

"But I *did*! My mother posted it for me."

"I never received it. I waited day after day and still no letter. I couldn't even phone or write to you! I assumed that you'd met someone else or that you just didn't love me anymore."

"After writing letter after letter and not hearing from you, I thought it was *you* that didn't love me. I waited and waited! You broke my heart, Simon."

"I didn't get one letter, Mary. So what happened to them?"

"My mother!" she gasped. "How could she? I can't believe she would do that!" She explained to Simon that on the car journey her mother had said that she was too young to be tied and that she would soon forget him. She had said that long-distance relationships didn't work and that it would be better not to write.

"But I told her how much I loved you and that I wanted to write to you. She even *agreed* and said that of course it was up to me! I cannot believe she would do such a thing to me - not posting my letters! How could she? She even lied to me when I asked her if she had posted all of them!" she cried out.

"It doesn't matter now, Mary. The important thing is we found each other again," he said hugging her to him.

Simon married Mary as soon as he could, in fear of fate separating them again. The love they shared was worth more to him than any riches, for Mary was his soul mate.

They would spend the long summer holidays catching the train to the coast to their favourite cliff-top, where they would walk hand-in-hand. Several times a day he would say, "Love you," and she would say, "I love you too." As the years passed their love grew stronger and they couldn't bear to be parted again.

It was their anniversary and, as usual, they went to their special place, the cliff-top walk. Because Simon knew it meant more to Mary than any gift he could give her, he wanted it to be extra special. So, with careful planning, he timed it to get there as the sun was going down over the sea. It was always a beautiful sight, but somehow this time it was even more breathtaking. It was as though someone had painted the sky with streaks of dusky pink and magenta just for them. The same hand had placed   the red sun in position, dipping below the horizon, its reflection glittering on the water and making the sea's white horses dance for them to the rhythm of the waves.   It was as if the artist knew it was their anniversary; even the seagulls seemed to be calling a song to them.

Simon and Mary sat at the edge of the cliff holding hands, gazing out to sea. The sun had almost gone down and, although they didn't want it to end, they knew it would soon be getting late.

Simon stood and gave Mary his hand to help her up. As Mary was getting up, the clump of ground beneath her foot gave way. In the blink of an eye, Mary was hanging over the cliff edge, holding on by one hand to Simon's.

"I've got you!" Simon cried out.

He turned his head to see if there was anyone to help but, because it was so late, everyone else had gone home and even if he'd had his phone with him he couldn't have used it without letting go.

Simon's arm began to ache excruciatingly under the strain.   He tried to pull Mary up but every time she managed to get a foothold on the cliff it would give way, the sudden jerk causing unbearable pain in his arm.

Time seemed to stand still and all he could do was look down into Mary's eyes, assuring her fervently that it was going to be alright.   Yet, where he would have expected to see fear, he only saw love in her eyes. The strength in his arm was slowly going and his body was racked with pain and bathed in sweat.

Mary could tell what she was doing to him. With the words, "Simon, I love you," she loosened the grip on his hand, until their fingertips gradually slipped apart and she was gone.

Simon stayed there a long time in shock. With tears in his eyes and too numb to move, the words, 'I love you' echoed in his head.

How could such a special day end this way; and how could fate be so cruel and separate them once more? His mind tormented him further over the fact that, in that moment of panic, he didn't say, "I love you," when Mary had said it to him. His life now lay at the bottom of the cliff.

As the months passed Simon found life without Mary hard to bear. Everything around him reminded him of her. He gave up his job and decided to travel the country. He wasn't sure what he was looking for. A part of him wanted to find love again, another was telling him that if he didn't find love, he couldn't lose it. He decided once again to leave it to whatever fate had in store for him.

Travelling, and not working, soon took a toll on his money. All he had left was the wristwatch that Mary had bought him on their anniversary and, as painful as it was to part with it, he decided to sell it to pay for a train ticket to the coast, to the ill-fated cliff-top that had haunted him day and night. The train was quite empty, which gave him a seat by the window. Before long his head was resting on the window glass and his eyes were becoming heavy. He fought against it, but every time he closed his eyes all he could see were Mary's eyes looking up at him as she said her final words, "Simon, I love you." He was exhausted from a lack of decent sleep since that day. As he began to drift in and out of sleep, not only was he seeing Mary's eyes but he could hear the words, "I love you," "I love you too." Then there began a rhythm to it.

First there would be slowly, "I love you," then slightly faster, "Love you too." It was the rhythm of the train wheels on the tracks attaching themselves to the words in his mind. It was sad and painful but mercifully sleep overtook him.

There was a sudden jolt, and the words. "All change! End of the line!" suddenly woke him up. He had slept past his stop. Peering out of the window, he couldn't make out where he was and he was the only one left in the carriage. Hoping to find someone on the station to ask was futile - it was an unmanned station. Even the name on the hanging board, 'Salvation Halt', didn't help to tell him where he was. He couldn't make up his mind whether to stay on the train and go back to where he was supposed to get off, or walk through the station gate to an unknown place. He decided, because it must have been fate that he missed his stop, on the latter. Once outside he could see why it was the end of the line.

There was nothing but fields around with woods in the distance. The gravel path of the station forecourt led to the start of a lane. Having no choice he followed the lane for some distance until he came to a fork. The left fork continued on as a lane, but he could see that the right fork led into a track through the woods. As he stood there unsure which to take, as clearly as if someone was speaking next to him, he could hear a voice say, "Let's find out where this leads."

"Mary?" Simon said out loud.

Those words sent him back to when he and Mary loved exploring new places, especially when they were walking in the woods. She would say when they came across a track: "Lets find out where that leads!" Mary's voice made up his mind to take the track.

43

As he entered the woods he heard the sky rumble, and it turned dark. There wasn't much light even in daytime and now it was difficult to see where the track went.

Simon didn't have a clue where he was. He decided it would be better if he found somewhere to rest for the night and wait until it was light, giving him a better chance of finding his way, or wherever fate was to take him.

He found a large log set back from the track and decided it would be as good a place as any. As he sat on the ground with his back to the log a large black crow flew down from the tree and settled at his feet.

"Hello there!" he said as he reached out his hand to touch the crow.

As he did so the crow pecked him, drawing blood from his hand. Simon reacted by trying to kick it away but instantly several other crows flew down and started to attack him. He got to his feet and tried to fight off the crows with a branch but, as if he was their favourite prey, other crows flew down and joined in.

Realising there were too many to fight off, Simon ran further into the woods. He could see ahead that there was a very tall tree with extra-wide girth, covered in a thick overgrowth of black ivy. The crows were to his left, right and behind him and if he tried to run in either direction they would attack. If he slowed down the crows behind would peck him with their sharp beaks. He couldn't go in any direction but towards the tree. To his amazement, when he stopped at the tree the crows flew upwards settling in the branches high above. It was as if they had for some reason steered him there on purpose.

Knowing he had to rest somewhere, he settled down with his back to the tree, pretty sure that if he tried to move away the crows would attack him again. He could hear them above him in the trees, calling excitedly. His eyes started to get heavy again and he tried to keep them from closing but, in that sleepy state, his mind started to play tricks on him. The calling of the crows had turned into the calling of owls in the dark canopy of the trees and instead of hearing the normal sound of "Wooh" from the owls, Simon was hearing, "I wooh you," and the other owl was calling back, "I wooh you too." This went on for what seemed like hours. *Is there no rest for me?* he thought wretchedly. What was worse, it seemed he was a prisoner of the dark woods with no escape. He longed for peace yet the 'owls' were a constant reminder of his beloved Mary's words, "I love you".

Abruptly the noise of the owls stopped. Not a sound could be heard and it was as if he was the only living thing there. Then suddenly the silence was broken by the sound of hundreds of crows flapping their wings in the canopy of the trees as if they were applauding something that was coming.

Simon could see from his left an eerie blue mist rolling its way towards him from the depth of the woods. As it came closer he could see the mist was changing into a dark, dense fog that would soon be upon him.

His instinct was telling him to get out of the woods. Taking heed of the warning, he quickly got to his feet, when he heard "Simon, Simon!" It was a voice calling him from within the fog. He knew that voice. It made him turn around. Standing there in the fog was Mary.

In shock and disbelief he called softly, "Mary?"

"Yes, Simon, come to me."

Because Simon's heart longed to be with her so much, he found himself walking towards the fog. But, as he did so, he was distracted. Were his eyes playing tricks on him? A flickering light from his right in the distance was there and then gone.

It must be my imagination, he thought. *No, there it is again.*

This time it was not flickering. It seemed to be getting brighter and closer.

"Simon, come! If you want to be with me you must come quickly!" Mary said, causing him to turn and face her again.

In an instant the whole track and the trees were engulfed in brilliant light, driving the fog back from him, and separating him from the figure of Mary. All Simon could hear was her voice, still calling him to her, as she faded back into the fog from where she had come.

The light had Simon's full attention. He put a hand over his eyes to shield them from the dazzling effect. He could make out in the haze the shape of someone on a bicycle but, because of the intensity of the light, he couldn't see the person clearly. The figure was cocooned in the light. The bicycle stopped when it reached him.

Not knowing what to expect, Simon was ready to run. Then out of the light a voice said, "Simon, I have come to calm the storms in your mind. If you come with me and trust in me, I will give you what you are searching for: peace, and love and life. Without me you will always have an unquenchable thirst for the love you seek."

The voice seemed to have authority but was reassuring and kind.

Simon thought: *All this must be the result of my depression*. He had attended counselling sessions after Mary died and knew the effects that depression could have on a person. He hadn't finished the sessions and wondered if this was the result.

He didn't know if what he was seeing was real, but hoped it wasn't. He shut his eyes, hoping that when he opened them again whatever was there would end the confusion. As his eyelids started to open he could see the bright light was still there.

"Trust me, Simon, what you are seeing is real. Choose life and step into the light."

Even though he still didn't know if this was reality or the depression, a sense of calmness came upon him

What do I have to lose? Wherever I'm taken has got to be better than being trapped here with these crows and my mind playing tricks on me. Maybe I did manage to fall asleep and this is all a dream. Anyway, dreaming or not, I'm going to let fate decide.

He walked into the sphere of light and found himself on the back of the bike but, as close as he was, he still couldn't see the person in front. There was a wall of light that was separating them.

The bicycle moved off. Simon found that he didn't have anywhere to put his feet, but, before he could ask, the voice said, "There are no pedals. Sit back and let me do all the work."

How did he know what I was thinking? Simon thought.

He did what the voice said and, in a strange way, was enjoying himself. It had been a long time since he had done that.

His thoughts went back to when he and Mary had hired a tandem one holiday and had great fun travelling around. He could hear Mary's voice shouting, "Faster Simon, faster!" To which he would reply, "We would go faster if you pedalled instead of putting your feet up!" At that he would hear her laugh.

47

Just as his thoughts were taking him deeper into the past, the bicycle stopped.

"Simon, this is where you will find what you are looking for."

He found himself outside an inn. Laughter and singing were coming from inside. He dismounted from the bicycle and, even more confused, said, "Thanks for the lift."

Then it dawned on him. *How did he know my name?* But before he could ask, the voice said, moving off, "I've always known you, Simon and, before you ask, my name is Love."

Simon stood there for a moment, not knowing what to say or think as he watched the bicycle disappear along the track. He decided that the only logical explanation for what had just happened was that it had to have been a dream. But then how did he get to the inn. Was he still dreaming?

He went inside. Looking around he could see groups of people enjoying themselves. *They must be celebrating something,* he thought.

He noticed an old, white-bearded man smiling at him behind the bar with a drink in his outstretched hand. Simon made his way over to him and the old man handed him the drink.

"Welcome, Simon, we have been expecting you. Take a seat."

He sat down at the bar. *How come everyone knows my name?* he thought. *This is beyond weird!*

He started to look around at everyone there. He couldn't help noticing that all the people were in different period clothes, except for a man and a woman sitting together at a table in deep conversation. There was something about the woman that drew Simon's eyes and he kept looking at her. She must have sensed that someone was staring and she stopped talking and looked over at Simon.

Their eyes locked. She smiled and said, "Would you like to join us?"

Simon accepted her invitation. "Sorry, I was staring."

"That's okay. You look lost," said the woman.

"Sort of," said Simon. He couldn't help thinking that the woman's eyes reminded him of his dead wife's eyes.

"Simon Peters," he said, introducing himself.

"I'm Esther, and this is John."

Simon was surprised that they didn't ask where he was from or how he came to be there, as it was a remote place for a stranger to be.

As the evening went on, he felt very relaxed in his newfound company. Because most of the conversation was between him and Esther, Simon became concerned over whether he was coming between Esther and John, as it was the last thing he wanted to do. He decided to be frank.

"Are you two together?" he asked.

"Oh no, we only met this evening," they said, laughing because they both spoke at once.

Simon knew that there was something drawing him to Esther and he could sense that she felt the same. It seemed that the empty hole in his heart was already beginning to mend and if it was all a dream, he thought to himself, he was going to enjoy it.

Chapter four

The Deceiver

Next to speak was a heavily built man with a trim beard, who went by the name of Matthew Jameson, and was a stockbroker in the city. He had had an expensive lifestyle, fuelled by money he had made investing on the stock market. Matthew never gave anything away and would always be quick to take anything that was free. Where money was concerned he was ruthless. The wealth he had accumulated bought him expensive cars, clothes and a penthouse apartment. In fact, his god was money and it was greed that would be his downfall.

His avarice and over-confidence led him to make a bad investment, which ended up costing him most of the capital he needed to keep the funds coming in. With his head in both hands he studied the money market on the computer. He knew he had to do something or he would lose the lifestyle he was used to.

He approached many of his friends, saying that he had been told of a hot tip that could treble their investment, but they would have to be quick in making up their minds as the deal wouldn't last much longer.

Because his friends knew that he was successful in all of his investments, they trusted him with their money to invest as he saw fit. He worded the offer to them in such a way that they even thanked him for thinking of them. Little did they know that his idea involved using their money for his own gain. He even planned what to say to reassure them if they asked how their investments were doing; he would lie and say, "Not very well at the moment - the money market is down, give it a little longer and it will turn around."

He continued month after month with the same excuses until one of his friends said that he wanted his money back. Matthew said he would arrange it but that it would take time.

He knew it was only a matter of time before his friends found out the truth, which left him with a choice: to stay and face them and eventually the police, or empty his bank account and start over again in another city.

After a sleepless night he came to the decision to disappear. So in the early hours of the morning he closed the door behind him. He knew the police could trace him by the personalised registration on his red Ferrari, which drew attention wherever he went in it. As a part of the plan he had to abandon it, which didn't bother him as he always leased his cars. He drove to another city, parked the car in a quiet side road and left by train.

Although his original plan was to start again in some other city, he decided the countryside would be a better place to lose himself. All his friends knew he loved city life and would never expect to find him there. In some ways he was looking forward to it, as he hadn't been to the country since he was a boy. From a random choice of stations, he would choose the destination by its remoteness.

After several hours of travelling, and inspecting every stop, he found such a station. 'Salvation Halt.' It was the last stop on the line. Looking out of the window he noticed that no one was boarding the train or getting off. Deciding that this place was quiet enough, he left the train.

Making his way outside, he saw that there was just a lane that led into the forecourt of the station. And to his surprise there was a taxi waiting. He couldn't help wondering what it was doing there, unless it was to pick up someone who'd booked it. He made his way to the taxi and said to the driver, "Are you for hire or are you waiting for someone?"

The driver answered with a chuckle in his voice, "As there's nobody else here, it looks as though it's you I've been sent to pick up."

Matthew questioned him as to who sent him as nobody could have possibly known that he would be there.

The driver replied "My Boss."

Without questioning the driver's reply, Matthew thought, *He's got me mixed up with someone else and he's picking up the wrong person.* He got into the taxi, deliberately sitting in the back so as not to make conversation. However, he soon found himself asking, "Is this station always as deserted as this?"

"Mostly, but every now and again I'm sent to pick up someone, and you are just one more on the list," said the driver.

Matthew noted the word 'list', as it seemed to imply someone did know that he was coming.

The words, "So where to?" from the driver brought him out of his thoughts.

"Any place that's quiet and I can find somewhere to stay."

"I know just the place - a quiet pub that lets out rooms."

"Sounds great," said Matthew.

As he sat there, he was mesmerised by the cross on a chain that was swinging to and fro from the interior mirror. It wasn't long before they arrived and it was just as the taxi driver said, a typical country pub all on its own.

He paid the driver, who said, "Don't forget to mention that James recommended it to you!" and drove off.

Matthew went inside.   Not only was the pub quiet outside, there was nobody inside either. He made his way to the bar and rang the bell.

He waited for what seemed like a long time but was probably only a few minutes. He was just about to go and look round the back, when a voice said, "What will it be?"

Matthew turned around. "I need a room if you have one?"

He remembered that the taxi driver had told him to mention his name. Maybe by doing that he would be well looked after. And most likely the taxi driver and the pub had an arrangement between them.

"The taxi driver said to say that James recommended this place to me."

"I don't know who this 'James' is, but people keep on telling me that he's recommended this place! I'll have to thank him if I ever find out," he said as he handed Matthew a key, pointing to the stairs.

After a restful night, he decided that he would need some new clothes as his city clothes would make him stand out in this rural setting. After breakfast he asked the landlord if there was anywhere nearby that he could buy a few things.

"That would be the town, about twenty minutes from here. I've got to go into town. If you like I can give you a lift."

On the journey he thought that he'd better try and make some sort of small talk. "How long have you been at the pub?"

"About ten years. It was good back then but, over the years, things seemed to go downhill, especially with losing my son. And, with very few people visiting, it's taken a toll on my finances. That's the reason I'm going into town - to see if the bank can help with some money."

Matthew wasn't really listening. He was thinking about what type of clothes he was going to buy, but the words 'bank' and 'money' made him pay attention. It wasn't long before they arrived at the town square.

"I will be about an hour. If you are done by then, meet me here and I'll give you a lift back."

Walking around the town, he could see he didn't have a choice of shops to buy clothes from. He was used to designer clothes shops, where he could have the best that money could buy. This was like going back fifty years, but he realised it would have to do if he wanted his plan to work.

Satisfied with his appearance, he decided to wear his new clothes out of the shop and had his old clothes put in a bag.

On the way back he passed a rubbish bin on the square and, having made sure no one was looking, he dropped the bag into it. No sooner had he walked a few paces than a down-and-out man retrieved it. Matthew didn't realize the old man had been watching him. He smiled to himself, thinking that the chap would probably never know how much those clothes had cost, and that they would make him the smartest and richest-looking person in town.

He hadn't walked far when the thought caused him to stop in his tracks. His hand went to his inside jacket pocket to check that he had taken his wallet from his old clothes before dumping them. With a sigh of relief he realised he had. Smiling, he made his way back to the square for his lift back.

"You look different. You look as if you're a local," said the landlord.

Matthew laughed. It was just what he wanted to hear. On the drive back the landlord didn't say anything and he didn't look happy.

"Everything all right?" asked Matthew.

"Not really. The bank said no," replied the landlord.

No to what? thought Matthew. Then he remembered why the landlord had gone into town. "That's a shame. What will you do now?"

"Don't know. Probably have to sell the old pub."

They soon arrived back at the inn.

That night, for the first time in his life, Matthew's worry was about someone other than himself. He had the landlord's problem on his mind as he lay on the bed. Because this feeling was completely new to him he was unable to sleep.

The morning came and he found himself at the breakfast table talking to the landlord about his problems and suggesting ways that might help.

As the days passed, Matthew found something strange happening. He had noticed that, all the time he was involved with someone else's problem, he wasn't thinking about his own. And what was more amazing was that he was quite enjoying it. He and the landlord were becoming quite good friends and fairly chatty. It wasn't something that he had intended to let happen and, for that reason, he knew it was time to move on. The week's stay soon came to an end.

He was in his room packing, when a thought came to him that he should help the landlord by giving him some money. Because this was totally out of character for him, he dismissed it and made his way to the door.

The thought repeated. Slowly turning the door handle to make his way out, he then heard an audible voice: "Give him some money." It made him let go of the door handle. He turned around and sat down on the bed, not knowing if what he had just heard was real or not. He found himself opening his bag and taking out a wad of notes, which he then put in a brown bag retrieved from the waste bin.

Where this newfound desire came from didn't matter. The only thing he knew deep inside was that he wanted to help his friend, by leaving him enough money to solve his problems.

He made his way down the stairs and found the landlord at the bar. "I'm leaving now. I'd like to settle the bill, and could you call me a taxi?"

The landlord seemed saddened that Matthew was moving on. He said, "I hope you've enjoyed your stay. I've enjoyed my talks with you, and thanks for the advice."

He presented Matthew with the bill. Looking at it, Matthew could see it was the cheapest week's stay he had ever had to pay for. With a word of thanks he made his way to the door.

"Keep in touch!" the landlord called out.

That evening when the landlord went to clean the room, he noticed a brown paper bag on the bed and a note. Unfolding the note, he read:

'Thank you for giving me the opportunity of doing something I've never done before. I have now found that there's more pleasure in giving than receiving. I know that you will find this of more use than me. Thanks again.

Matthew."

When he emptied the bag out on the bed he was shocked to find tens of thousands of pounds!

Matthew recognised the taxi driver. It was James who had picked him up at the station.

"Where to?"

"Another quiet village, please," said Matthew.

"Not quiet enough there?" quipped James.

"Yes, it was fine. I'm doing research on country villages." He used that as a cover story to explain why he was moving on, but really it was the fear of the police catching up with him. He knew if he stayed there any

57

longer than a week there would be a good chance of that happening.

"You say it's quiet villages you're looking for? Leave that to me. I've got just the place in mind, about an hour's drive away."

"I'm in no hurry. Take your time."

Matthew noticed a group of cottages they had just passed. "What was that place?" he asked.

"What place?" replied James.

"Back there."

"Oh, that. It used to be a stopping place for people passing through but since the village up ahead got its first guesthouse nobody stays there anymore, it's too quiet."

"Is there anywhere to stay then?"

"One of the cottages used to let out a room, but I don't know about now. There is a small pub and a shop and that's it."

"Stop! Turn around – it's what I'm looking for," said Matthew.

"Are you sure? It's so dead, people who live there can't wait to leave," answered James.

"I'm sure!"

The taxi driver stopped outside the pub. Matthew paid him.

"Have fun!" he said, laughing as he drove off.

Matthew went into the pub. *He was right*, he thought, *you could hear a pin drop.* "Hello!" he called out.

"Coming!" a voice replied. "Sorry about that, I was out the back. What can I do for you?" said the owner.

"I'm looking for somewhere to stay," Matthew replied.

The owner, with a surprised look on his face, said: "It's been a long time since anybody asked that! The only place around here is at 'Rahab Hide Cottage,' two cottages up on the right. Abigail Nun, she does bed and breakfast." Matthew thanked him and went off to find the cottage.

Sure enough, on the front of the gate was the name 'Rahab Hide Cottage'. He thought the name said it all.

He knocked on the door, to be greeted by a young woman with a look of surprise on her face. Matthew stood there stunned by her beauty. "The chap at the pub said you let rooms out."

"I don't know about rooms. I have only a small attic room."

"That sounds fine. My name is Matthew Jameson."

"Abigail Nun, but I like Abi. Sorry if I seemed surprised, it's that we don't get as many people around here as we used to," she said, showing him to the room. "Well this is it. As I said, it's only an attic room."

"It's more than enough for my stay."

"How long do you think that will be?"

"Not quite sure - probably a week or so."

"Well, I hope you enjoy your stay. We don't have much here, but please feel free to come down and watch the TV if you want to."

"Thank you!" Matthew replied.

In the morning he made his way downstairs to the smell of eggs and bacon.

"Did you sleep well?"

"Yes, thank you," he replied.

"I hope you like eggs and bacon."

"Great!" The last time he had that was in his teens when he lived at home and his mother had cooked for him.

The door opened and a young lad came in yawning.

"Morning lazy bones. This is Samuel, my son."

"Hello, I'm Matthew." He noticed Samuel was a frail and pale-looking lad. Samuel didn't say anything. His mother apologized and said, "He's not used to seeing anyone here; he's a little shy but once he gets to know you he'll be fine. He likes to be called Sam."

"Is there a Mr. Nun?" Matthew asked.

With sadness in her voice, she replied, "No, he passed away last year."

Matthew wished he had never asked.

"It's been tough since we lost David and everything seems to have got worse, what with Sam's illness.

"What's wrong with him?"

"Sam's always suffered with a weak chest and the shock of losing his dad made him ill. I nearly lost him with pneumonia. The hospital said I should take him somewhere warm and sunny this winter but it's not so easy, what with trying to make ends meet, being a single mum, even with the extra income from cleaning at the pub."

"I'm sure things will get better for you," Matthew said, trying to lighten the conversation. "So what is there to do around here?" he asked.

"Let me see. There are the fields and more fields. Oh, and the woods," she laughed.

"Quite a bit to do then?" Matthew said smiling.

"David and I used to have lovely walks through the woods to the river where we would have a picnic. It's so peaceful, we could have stayed there all day. On weekends David used to take Sam there to fish."

Matthew's mind went back to when he was a boy. He always wanted his father to take him fishing but he was always too busy with work. Matthew grew up not having that special father and son relationship. "How far is the river?"

"Not far. It's the other side of the field," replied Abi.

"I think I'll have a wander to the river after breakfast."

"It will be nice there this time of year," she said.

Matthew spent an hour sitting on the riverbank, listening to the water tumbling over the rocks. The tranquil sound of the water compared to the stress and noise of the city was so peaceful. It was like two different worlds. Here he felt free from all that the city had to offer. *Why would I want to go back, when I can have this new relaxed life?* he thought to himself.

"Was it as nice as I said?" Abi asked.

"Yes! I can see what you mean about the peace. It's priceless. I might go back there tomorrow."

"Let me know and I'll pack you a lunch."

"Thank you. I might take you up on that."

"My pleasure," replied Abi.

After breakfast the next morning, Matthew said that he was going to the river again and, as it was Saturday, he asked Abi if Sam would like to go fishing. He was half-expecting her to say no because she didn't really know him, but she said,

"Sam, would you like to go fishing with Matthew?"

Sam's eyes lit up. "Can I?"

"If you want to," his mother said.

Sam ran off to get his fishing rod.

Abi, who was observant, noticed that Matthew wasn't wearing his wristwatch and said, "You've forgotten your watch."

"I've left it off on purpose. When we are hungry it will be time to come home."

"I'm sure Sam will let you know if food's the judge," said Abi. "Don't forget your coat!" she called out to Sam.

"Yes, Mum!"

They made their way to the river. For a shy boy, Sam didn't stop talking about how much he had loved his time with his dad fishing. He told how they would sit on the riverbank where his dad would tell him stories of the river. Matthew could hear the excitement in Sam's voice as he spoke.

"Dad said that there was gold in the river. He told me that at certain times, when the sun was shining in a certain direction, you could see the gold glinting on the riverbed. The gold in the river has been flowing down from the hills of 'Valhiah' since the beginning of time, so Dad said."

"'Valhiah?' That's a strange name," Matthew said.

"Valhiah' was a land full of precious jewels and gold," Sam went on to say.

To keep his excitement going Matthew asked, "What's the name of the river?"

"Shipon,' Sam replied.

"So the land is called 'Valhiah' and the river 'Shipon?' They're strange names, Sam."

"When Dad told me the story I said that to him."

"What did he say?"

"He said that to reveal the mystery of the names you had to unjumble the letters. I tried but could never do it. I used to say, "Dad give me a clue," but all he would do was give me a piece of paper with some letters on it and numbers, and say: "Read your Bible!" I would read it in bed every night before going to sleep hoping, as Dad sat there, he would show me where to search."

"And did he?"

Matthew could see a little tear in Sam's eyes starting to form. "Dad said he would show me one day, but he died. I gave up looking and haven't opened it since."

Sam went on to say how much he had missed the stories and the fishing since his dad had gone and how, every night before he went to sleep, he would pray that God would send someone to take him fishing again.

As Matthew listened to Sam, the words: "The faith of a child prevails" came to his mind. He could see, through Sam's excitement, what it would have been like if his father had taken him fishing when he was a boy, and how he envied Sam having a story to tell.

"I've got one!" Sam shouted.

It was a big fish. "So, it's fish for supper!" Matthew said.

"Mum will be pleased!" Sam said excitedly. "Let's go back and show her!"

Sam ran on ahead with the fish, leaving Matthew to carry the rod.

As he made his way through the door, he could hear Sam telling his mother what a great time he'd had.

"Thanks, Matthew. It's been a long time since I've seen Sam excited like that and he's even got a bit of colour in his cheeks. I'm going to make fish pie. Will you have supper with us?"

"I would love to," Matthew said with a smile on his face. As a bachelor, he was used to having meals on his own and now he was experiencing sitting around a table partaking in family life. This was new to him and he liked it.

After supper Matthew said, "Sam, go and find that bit of paper with the letters and numbers on and bring your

Bible. We'll see if we can unscramble the words and find the real names of Valhiah and Shipon."

As Sam went off, Abi said, "What bit of paper is that?"

"Sam was telling me the story of the land of Valhiah, filled with gold, and that it flowed into the river Shipon, and the only clue he had to reveal the real names was on a piece of paper that his dad gave him."

"I can see you can't resist a mystery. That was Sam's favourite story of all the ones his dad told him. It was David's way of keeping Sam reading his Bible every night. His dad was good at making up stories."

Matthew smiled and thought, "She was right about me liking a good mystery. The truth was - yes, he thought it would be good for Sam to find out about the names, but he wanted to know as well.

Sam came running down the stairs, missing every other step, with a Bible in his hand and the piece of paper.

"Slow down, Sam!" his mother said.

Sam drew his seat close to Matthew and gave him the piece of paper.

Reading the letters and numbers and opening the Bible, Matthew said, "Gen 2: 11. It's the book of Genesis, chapter 2, verse 11." Matthew read out the scripture from the book. "It's talking about four rivers," he said. "The name of the first is: Pishon - it winds through the entire land of Havilah, where there is gold. So if we unscramble the letters of 'Shipon' we have 'Pishon' and 'Valhiah' we have 'Havilah'. So there we have it, Sam, mystery solved!"

"Wow, Mum the story's true. It was there all the time in the Bible and Dad knew it!"

"Yes, Sam, he did. I think you have had enough excitement for the day. It's bedtime now. Thank Matthew and say goodnight to him."

"Do I have to, Mum? I'm not tired."

Matthew, who could see that Abi was going to have trouble getting Sam upstairs, said, "I'll tell you what, Sam, if you hurry up to bed, I might take you fishing again - if that's okay with Mum." To Matthew's surprise, Sam gave him a big hug and thanked him for the day before he hurried away upstairs.

"It was really good of you to do that for Sam. I can see he's getting attached to you."

Matthew felt the same way about Sam.

Abi continued, "In some ways I'm a little sad that the riddle of the river has been solved. I know he wanted to know the mystery of the names but I'm concerned that it was the only thing Sam had left from his dad and now he might miss it."

"Sorry about that, Abi. I suppose there's always a mixture of happiness and sadness when a mystery's been solved, but I'm sure, from the little amount of time I've known Sam, that he's a boy who will always be on the trail of a new mystery. By the way, what is the real name of the river?"

"I think it's named after this area – 'Eden'.

Matthew found himself spending the weekends and sometimes after school with Sam at the river, fishing. One day, while Sam was at school, he decided to have one more trip to the river. He was just sitting on the bank gazing into the water when, for a split second, the sun broke through the trees and shone across the water. He had to look twice. The riverbed had a sparkle of gold!

Smiling, he said to himself, "I can see where Sam's dad got the story from now!"

Thinking about Sam, he began to realise that, because he was getting too attached to him and his newfound experience of family life, he would soon have to go, so he decided that tomorrow would be his last day. Half of him wanted to stay but the other half knew he had to move on.

With sadness in his voice, that night at the meal table he told Abi and Sam that he had to leave.

The morning soon arrived. After paying for his room he said goodbye to Abi and Sam and they waved to him from the doorway. Walking down the lane he heard quick footsteps behind him. It was Sam running after him.

As Matthew stopped to turn round, Sam threw his arms around him saying, "Don't leave, please don't go!"

Even in childhood, Matthew had never known the feeling of being wanted. "Sam!" he said, "I have to go, but I will come back one day, I promise you, and we will go back to the river and find that gold."

"You promise?"

"I promise, Sam."

Sam made his way back to his mother, who was watching from the door.

Matthew glanced once more over his shoulder at them both.

He decided to travel on foot to the next village.

Later that day, Abi went into Matthew's room to clean it. The first thing she noticed was a note with her name on beside a package on the bed. The note said,

' Just a little something to say thank you for giving me the opportunity to experience what it's like to be part of a family. With all my money there is so much I could buy in life, but what I've found here I could not buy. I have always been governed by time, but now I have found that time isn't important. Please accept this little gift of my wristwatch and money - use it to take Sam on the holiday he needs. Once again, thank you.
Matthew.'

When Abi saw how much money was in the package, and the make of the watch (which was worth a small fortune in itself), she burst into tears.

Matthew enjoyed the beauty of the countryside as he walked. He thought he had a good idea of the direction of the village from what the taxi driver had told him but, after an hour of walking, he realised some of the landmarks were familiar. He had been going round in a circle! And, as it was getting late and the sun was going down, he knew he had to find the way soon before it was dark.

Luck was on his side. A tractor was coming up the lane behind him.

"Afternoon," said the farmer as he drove past.

"Excuse me!" shouted Matthew. "Can you tell me the way to the village? Is it far?"

The tractor stopped. At the wheel was an old, bearded guy with a wide-rimmed, floppy hat worn over long white hair, which gave him the appearance of being far too old to be driving a tractor. "Not too far. It's over the next hill; turn left after the river bridge. Matter of fact, I'm going that way. 'Op on and I'll give you a lift."

"No thanks. I'm enjoying the walk." He said that, as he felt he wouldn't be safe with someone so old driving. Matthew watched the tractor drive off erratically.

He realized where he had gone wrong. He had turned right after the bridge. It wasn't long before he found the bridge again. *Turn left*, he remembered.

By now the light had almost gone and mist was forming on the ground and, to make things worse, he could see by the black clouds forming that there was a storm coming his way.

It was getting hard to see and there didn't seem to be any signposts for the village. He couldn't make out where he had gone wrong again. He kept going over the directions the tractor driver gave him. He kept walking till he came to a fork in the lane.

The rain had started to fall and he could hear the heavens rumbling. He was now faced with a choice: to carry on up the lane or turn right into a wooded track to wait out the storm. The crack of thunder and the heaviness of the rain made the decision for him and he ran into the shelter of the woods.

Nearly an hour had passed. Standing at the entrance of the woods, he could see by the darkness of the sky that it would be some time before the rain would stop. Looking around, he saw that the track through the woods ran parallel to the lane outside that supposedly led to the village. He decided to carry on along the track, hoping it would lead him to the village and, worst scenario: if he had to stop for the night he could use the shelter of the woods.

Making his way along the track, he could hear the faint murmur of the wind in the leaves high above. He was amazed at how muffled the sound was; it was as though the storm was shut out of this place.

The eeriness caused his mind to drift back to his early teens when he and his friends spent a weekend camping in the woods. He remembered the trick he played on two of his friends in the early hours of the night as they slept in their tent. He had already planned the trick before he had left home. He knew, for it to work, he had to create an atmosphere around the fire before they went to sleep.

He started to tell them a story, saying that in the woods there had been a grizzly murder. A body was found but the head was missing. He told them that it was rumoured that the woods were haunted by a headless person roaming the woods and, on certain nights when there was a full moon, it was said that you could hear him moaning and searching for his head.

When he was confident that they were asleep, he and his other friend went over to their tent and the two of them made groaning noises outside, followed by a high pitched scream. He then tossed into the tent a bone with some meat hanging from it.   As they crept back, they stifled their laughter at the screams and commotion, then slithered into their own tent and pretended to be asleep. The trick backfired on him as he spent a cramped night with four of them sleeping in a two-man tent, despite repeatedly telling them that it was a joke!

The track had become a tunnel of trees letting small amounts of rain through. But the further he went into the tunnel, the denser and darker the canopy of foliage got, until there was no rain at all. The silence was suddenly broken by a howling wind blowing through the trees.

Up ahead was a vortex of bluish, thick fog that was coming down the tunnel of trees towards him. Horrified, he turned around to go back but, as he did so, a flock of black crows swooped down, circling him. Trying to avoid them, he ran off into the trees, hoping they would not follow him but in the dark mist something tripped him. The next thing he knew he was on the ground with his head hurting.

He managed to prop himself up with his back against a tree, unable to move because of dizziness. The pain in his head was telling him to sleep, but he knew he had to stay awake. He found that he was unable to move his legs and, looking down in disbelief, he could see the reason why.

A thick strand of black ivy had coiled itself round his ankles and was creeping up around his body, tightening its grip. In his haste to get away from the crows, he hadn't noticed that the floor of the woods was covered in it. It wasn't normal ivy - every strand was alive, raising its tendrils upwards, searching for prey to entrap. In desperation, he knew he had to get free before it was around his arms or he wouldn't be able to stop it wrapping round his throat and choking him.

The more he tore the ivy away, the faster it grew back. He was losing the battle as both arms were held fast and it started to wind its way, strand by strand, around his throat. All he could manage was a weak croak of "Help!" that no one would hear before the life was squeezed out of him.

Almost unconscious, he could hear the sound of a distant bell that made him come to enough to open his eyes, and to see a faint light in the darkness. He tried to focus but the blood from his head wound trickling into his eyes was making it hard to see. Gasping for air, he felt a glimmer of hope as the light could possibly mean that someone would find him.

As if an evil force controlling the ivy, or something else in the woods, was reading his thoughts, from the base of the tree came a vortex of dense fog, almost shielding him from the light - but, because of its intensity, he could still see it piercing the darkness.

He could feel the grip of the ivy around him weakening, but not freeing him. Then from out of the light he heard, spoken with authority, the words: "Be gone!" The covering of fog instantly receded a short distance from Matthew.

In front of him he could see a pulsating light and, between the pulses, he thought he could see the shape of a person. "Be gone!" came the voice again.

Matthew could feel the ivy unwrap itself from his body and, with the fog, disappear back into the ground.

Still unable to see clearly because of the blood in his eyes, he heard the voice say, "It looks as though it's you who needs help now, Matthew."

I *must be in trouble* he said to himself. *This bang to my head must be more serious than I thought. I'm seeing things and hearing voices.*

He heard the voice again. "Matthew the darkness in these woods is waiting for you. Within it is death. I have come to give you life. Choose!"

Matthew could feel the ominous presence of darkness as it tried in vain to move towards him. Instead it seemed to swirl around, seething in anger. From somewhere came new strength to get up and, as though in a dream,

71

he found himself obeying the voice and choosing life as he made his way towards the light. He could see something materialising. It was the figure of a man.

"Come, Matthew don't take your eyes of me, take my hand."

As he did so, he could feel his head wound had completely healed.

"This way Matthew," the man said, putting his arm around Matthew's shoulders. "Whatever you do, don't look to the left or the right. Keep looking ahead. There is great evil all around that will try and take you from me."

Matthew found that he was cocooned in a sphere of white light as he walked along the track with the man. He could hear to his left and right the sound of crows cawing, as if they were communicating with each other, and the violent rustling of the vegetation that sounded as if it was alive. He noticed that the crows that came too close to the light were dropping dead. His thoughts went to his Ferrari; how he wished he were in it, with the speed to escape fast.

"Matthew, what use is a Ferrari to you now? Materialistic things have no meaning here. I am your hope in the darkness."

He knows my thoughts? Putting it to the test, he thought: *Why did the crows die when they came close?*

"Evil cannot stand in my presence," came the reply.

Matthew was lost for words. It wasn't long before they stopped. He could see they were outside what looked like an inn set back in the woods.

"Your new life starts here, Matthew," said the man.

Stepping out of the light, Matthew found himself outside the doors of the inn. All the time he had been in the sphere he had tried as hard as he could to see the face of the person but the light was too bright.

He said, "How do you know my name and who are you?"

The light seemed to intensify and started to move back into the woods; Matthew didn't think he was going to get an answer.

Then from out of the sphere the voice said, "I have always known you, Matthew. I am the generosity that now lives in you. What you did for the landlord, then for Abigail and her son, you did for me. You have chosen the life I have offered you. If you ever need anything, ask with the faith of a child, like Sam." With that the figure and the light surrounding him disappeared into the darkness.

Matthew, still confused at what had just happened, just stood outside the doors, staring into the dark woods.

The sound of someone laughing made him turn around towards the inn and make his way inside.

He looked quite a state with dried blood over his face. His attention was drawn to the smile of the white-bearded man behind the bar.

"Take a seat here, Matthew. We'll look after you," he said cheerfully.

Before he knew what was happening, a young girl appeared with a bowl of water and washed the blood from his face. Sitting there, he was thinking how strange it was that nobody was staring at him. They hadn't even turned to look as he came through the door. If this had been a scene in one of the Westerns he liked to watch, the place would have come to a standstill as the stranger walked in with blood on his face.

"How do you feel now, Matthew?" said the old man.

"Fine!" replied Matthew, distracted by the thought that there was something about the face of the old man that was familiar, although he couldn't recall where he had seen him before.

"This way!" the old man said, making his way round to the other side of the bar and escorting him over to where John, Esther and Simon were sitting. He introduced them.

As Matthew stood there, Esther said, "Fog, crows, light or tandem?"

"Err, how did you know?"

"They seem to be the norm around here."

"Give him a chance, Esther! Let him sit down - you can see he's confused, just as we were when we came here."

"I was only saying, John."

"Matthew isn't it? Let me get you a drink," John said, standing up.

Matthew sat there reflecting on what had taken place in the woods, knowing in his heart that he had been given another chance in life.

Chapter five

Abducted

The youngest person to tell her story was a pretty, young, red-haired girl with freckles, called 'Jessie Bell'. She looked as though she had been living rough, her clothes dirty and torn. She described how she had been brought up with a strictly religious background. Her father was a minister and her mother attended all the church services she possibly could and was always praying about everything, especially for her. Every Sunday she had had to go with her parents to church and she attended the weekly youth group. In her early teens she became rebellious towards her parents' strictness about attending church and not being able to do the things she wanted to do. On youth group evenings, she would deliberately turn up late and always leave early so she wouldn't be involved with the opening and closing prayer time.

At school she overheard her friends talking about a nightclub they had found. The thought of it excited her and she asked them about it.

"Why don't you come?" they urged her. Too embarrassed to tell them she had to go to church youth group, she replied, "What time?"

"We'll be there about 7.30. We'll look out for you."

"Okay," Jessie replied.

She knew that somehow she had to find a way to go now that she had said she would, as they would never let her forget it if she didn't.

She decided to act as though all was normal, saying to her parents that she would see them at the usual time, when the youth group meeting finished. As always, her mum said, "Enjoy yourself, and see you when you get back." Packing a change of clothes in her bag, she called out, "Bye Mum!" As she closed the door behind her, little did it occur to her that it was a decision that would lead her on a downward path she couldn't stop.

Outside the doors of the club, she could hear the loud music. Instantly she felt the excitement that she longed for and it was drawing her in. She made her way to the lobby toilets to quickly change into the clothes she'd brought with her. Going through the main doors, she could see that there was so much to take in. There were flashing lights in time with the loud music, and people were dancing in a frenzy, seemingly lost in another world. It wasn't long before she could feel her body responding to the rhythm of the music. It was all so thrilling and she knew this was the life she had longed for.

Over at a table in the corner she noticed her school friends drinking with a man who looked old enough to be their father. One of her friends saw Jessie standing there, and came over to her.

"You made it!" she said with surprise, as they had all been saying that she wouldn't turn up, based on the numerous times that they had asked her to go out with them and she had answered, "No, I can't."

Taking Jessie by the hand, her friend said, "Come over and see the girls and Nick."

"Who's Nick?" said Jessie hesitantly.

"He's great. He buys us all drinks. I'll introduce you to him."

Jessie was led to the table, where her life was about to change. She had never experienced alcohol before, and was soon tempted by her friends to have a drink. As the evening went on it soon began to take effect on her and she liked the feeling it gave her. Nick kept looking at her and as soon as her glass was empty, or those of her friends, he would buy them more.

"Where do you live, Jessie?" asked Nick.

Giggling, she said. "Here now."

"That's good," said Nick. To impress her, he said, "So do I. I own the club."

As the evening went on, the drink kept flowing and it didn't seem long before her friends said that it was 11 o'clock and that they were going home. They asked if she was going with them.

The youth club had finished long ago and her parents would already be phoning around to see where she was.

Jessie waved them good-bye, without any concerns about the time or that her parents would be worrying. She said drunkenly, "I'm okay. I'm enjoying myself! You go - I'll be all right. Nick will look after me, won't you, Nick?"

"Sure I will. I'll take care of her and make sure she get's home."

The girls left, having drunk too much themselves to be concerned about leaving her with Nick.

Hardly able to stand up, she said to Nick, "I have to go the Ladies'."

While she was away Nick took his opportunity. Making sure that nobody was watching, he took from his pocket a pill and put it in Jessie's drink.

Jessie woke up with an aching head to find that she wasn't in her own bed. She was confused and felt alarmingly different. Seeing that her clothes were on the floor, she got out of bed, dressed and went to the door. Turning the handle, she found that it was locked! On one wall of the room she could see a window with the curtains drawn. She quickly drew them aside to reveal that it was boarded up. In terror, she hammered on the door with her fists and began to shout. But nobody answered. Jessie sat back down on the bed, trying to control her fear. She had no idea where she was or how she had got there. All she could remember was going to the club, meeting her friends and enjoying herself, then nothing else. She hunted frantically for her phone but that, and her watch, were nowhere to be found.

She heard a key being put into the door, then it opened. It was Nick with a glass of water.

"Drink this. You'll feel better," he said.

"Who are you? How did I get here?" Then she remembered. He was the guy at the table with her friends, buying them all drinks.

"It was late. Your friends had all gone and you were in no fit state to go home alone, or for your parents to see you. Drink the water - it will make you feel better, then I'll take you home."

Jessie's mouth was dry and tasted awful. She drank the water eagerly, oblivious to the fact that it had another pill in it.

Before she had a chance to ask any more questions, Nick said, "I'll just bring the car round." He left, locking the door behind him.

Puzzled as to why he would lock the door, Jessie tried to get up to follow him. Still not completely over the effects of the first pill - which was now boosted by the second one, she felt dizzy and fell back down on the bed unable to move, yet she was able to hear the door being unlocked and voices talking, as she drifted into sleep.

When she came to, she found that she was in a different place, having no idea of the time or even what day it was. All that was in the room was a mattress with a dim light hanging from the ceiling. Again there were no windows. She was alone, scared and longed to be at home with her family where she felt secure and safe, but that seemed a long way from where she was now.

She could hear her mother's last words: "Enjoy yourself, and see you when you get back." *They must be worried out of their minds that I didn't come home*, she thought. They would certainly know by now that she hadn't gone to youth group.

The sound of the door being unlocked interrupted her thoughts, and two men came into the room. "Get up! And come!" ordered one of them.

She was shown to the bathroom and told to clean herself up and put on the clothes she was handed. Full of fear, she did what she was told. Although the clothes were a reasonable fit, they were far more revealing and provocative than she would ever dream of wearing. She felt so embarrassed and self-conscious that she hung back, afraid to leave the bathroom until she heard banging on the door and shouting at her to hurry up. When she came out one of the men grabbed her roughly by the arm and led her to another room, telling her to wait there. The door was again locked behind her.

After what seemed like hours, the key turned and a man she had never seen before came in. What happened next was to set her on a way of life that she had heard of, but never thought she would be a part of.

The days turned to months and months into years. Jessie never stopped thinking about her parents; the only comforting thought was that she knew her mother would never stop praying for her. Jessie's new life was ruled by fear; if she didn't do what was expected of her there would be beatings. She was made to work seven days a week, day and night. Drugs were a daily habit, which numbed her and helped with the things she had to do. She often thought about escaping when she was sent out to work at night on the streets but she was warned that she would be found and never see her family, or anyone else, again. If she didn't come home with enough money she would endure beatings and be subjected to things worse than she experienced on the street.

Jessie saw many new young girls come and go, and often wondered what happened to them when they didn't come back to the rooms. She often heard the cry of a girl in the next room, but never spoke with any of them as the girls were kept apart.

One night, while she was working on the streets, a white limo with blacked out windows pulled up alongside her.

The driver's window lowered. A voice said, "How much would you want for the night?"

Jessie had been told that she wasn't allowed to have anything to do with curb crawlers, and that any client she had was to be taken back to her room under the watchful eye of her minder. This was the first time that she had ever been approached by one but, because this car looked as if the owner had lots of money, she thought that there might be the slightest chance, however small, that she could escape, using the money she earned to get away.

She looked over to see if her minder was watching, but could see that he was at the end of the street having an argument with a man over one of the other girls. Using the opportunity, she walked over to the car. The rear door opened and, tempted by the thought of possible freedom, she got in.

She expected to see somebody in the back but there was only a driver in the car. All she could see of him was his back, which towered above the seat, his peaked cap almost touching the roof lining.

"Where are we going?" she asked.

The only response from the driver was a quick glance in the rear view mirror. Jessie swallowed and tried to fight the panic that was beginning to grip her. She regretted her impulsive decision and wondered if she was getting herself into an even worse situation. But then, it couldn't be that much worse, she told herself.

It wasn't long before the car pulled up in the underground car park of an apartment building. The driver got out and, opening the rear door without saying anything, beckoned her to follow him to a lift. Swiping a card so that the lift doors opened, the driver stepped to one side and instructed Jessie to go in. The lift moved swiftly upward. She started to count the floor indicator numbers as it ascended. One, two, three, four, five, six. But she soon lost count of the numbers as they flashed by. Suddenly the lift came to a gentle halt and the doors opened. She didn't know what to expect, but it wasn't what lay before her.

Walking out of the lift, she stepped into a large room that was furnished with many expensive items. There were white marble statues and gold-framed pictures on the walls, but there was no one in the room.

"Hello!" she called tentatively, but there was no answer.

In front of her were two open glass doors that led onto a balcony; and there on the balcony railing was a white dove looking at her. Slowly she made her way onto the balcony, hoping the dove wouldn't fly away. To her delight, it just sat there watching her. She reached out her hand to see how close she could get to it and, to her surprise, the dove hopped onto her hand.

"You're so beautiful!" she whispered.

The little dove, as if to say thank you in return, rubbed its head on her hand, giving her an wonderful feeling of peace. Deep in thought, she wished that she could fly away with the dove into the clouds, away from the life that held her captive.

The words: "You like the view?" made Jessie jolt her hand causing the dove to suddenly fly away, leaving a tiny white feather in her hand.

She turned around, to see a smartly dressed man. Nervously, she replied. "Yes, it must be great living up here - with all the birds."

"I've never thought of it like that. I just love the peace and being away from all the hustle and bustle of life, with my little friend."

"Little friend?"

"The dove that was sitting on your hand."

Jessie smiled.

"Sorry, I haven't introduced myself. I'm Michael."

"Jessie," she replied.

"Would you like a drink or something to eat?"

"Maybe a sandwich and some water, thank you," which was what she normally was given by her captors to eat.

"Is that all? I can get you anything you like; I've got champagne, wine, just name it."

Those words: 'Anything you like' took her back to the time when her Dad and Mum had taken her out to a restaurant for a special treat on her birthday. She had been able to choose whatever she wanted.

"So what will it be, Jessie?"

She was apprehensive that if she were to ask for something special she would be letting herself in for something she couldn't get out of. "No, a sandwich will be fine - and water. I don't like alcohol anyway, thank you."

"Maybe something later? I normally have something brought in to eat."

Taking a seat, she relaxed into the luxury of the deep, soft cushions. For a moment it made her think about all the things in the past she had to do with a man without any luxury involved. What more would be expected from her in this lavish setting?

He came back from the kitchen with the sandwich and a glass of water and placed it on the side table. Jessie could see that this man was different from all the rest in that his voice wasn't demanding like all the others, but gentle and quiet. He sat opposite her and just looked at her as she ate her sandwich.

She broke the silence and said, "As you are paying for my time, is there anything you'd like me to do?"

"There's no rush. We have all the time in the world."

Jessie had forgotten that he was paying for the night.

"I'd just like to sit here and enjoy the beautiful things of life."

Jessie felt a little embarrassed, but also flattered, as she had never considered herself to be one of the beautiful things in life, especially with her red hair and freckles, although her dad would often call her his beautiful Jessie.

"Did my driver treat you well?" he asked.

"Yes, he did, though he didn't say much," she answered, not knowing what else she could say.

"That's what I like about him. He's loyal and he does his job. He knows my taste in beauty."

"I couldn't help noticing all the paintings on the walls and statues. Are you a collector?" Jessie asked.

"More of a rescuer and restorer. If I hear of someone, or something, that needs restoring I send my driver to bring them here."

"You used the word 'someone'. I can understand some**thing**, but how do you restore some**one**?"

"You'd be surprised, Jessie, how many people there are that need rescuing and restoring, one way or another. Take that bird you were looking at. I bet you were wishing that you were like him, able to fly free from what has been

84

holding you captive? That's what I try and do for people - set them free."

Jessie looked at him, not understanding what he meant. She thought: *How did he know what I was thinking about the dove?*

Changing the subject, he said, "Feel free to have a look around. You can have a freshen up in the bathroom if you like. Take a bath or shower. Help yourself."

The thought of a long, hot bath! She heard herself say, "I must confess a bath would be great."

"There are fresh towels and a robe in there and a lock on the door if you need it."

The words 'a lock' made her relax and she made her way to the bathroom. Opening the door, she almost gasped. She had never seen such luxury before. The walls and floor were covered in white marble with gold veins running through and the bath was huge with massage jets and gold fittings. As she started running the water, she noticed that on the glass shelf was a range of scented soaps that she could add to the water. She took her time opening each bottle to smell the perfume then she poured a little from every bottle, and relaxed in the fragrant bubbles. As she lay there she realised that, in her excitement, she had not locked the door.

"Are you okay in there?" a voice from outside the door called.

She instantly tried to reach for the towel as she was expecting to see the doorknob turn. She replied guardedly, "I'm fine, thank you."

The words: "Take your time. I'll be in the other room when you are finished," meant she could relax, at least for a while.

Dressed in the white robe, Jessie made her way to the main room expecting to do what she had been brought there for, but was confronted by a table laid out with food. Her eyes went to a little bunch of yellow flowers in the centre of the table.

Michael, appearing from the other room, said, "Feeling refreshed? I thought you would be hungry now and had some food brought in."

Jessie, a little overwhelmed, didn't know what to say. She sat down and began to eat. She hadn't tasted food like it, even when she was at home and she tried a little of each dish set before her. It wasn't long before the automatic curtains drew themselves because of the darkness outside. Even though Michael, up to this point, hadn't demanded anything from her, now it was dark she was expecting him to. As she feared, Michael stood up, took her hand to help her out of the chair and led her to the bedroom.

"This is your room, Jessie. I will probably be gone when you wake up. There's no rush for you to leave. Help yourself to food."

"I thought this was where you were going to sleep as well."

Closing the door, Michael said, "No, Jessie, I only need one day a week's rest. I have my own room. God bless."

Those words brought back memories of home, of her mum and dad who would put their heads around the bedroom door to say, "Good night, God bless."

Confused, Jessie soon fell into a deep sleep.

She awoke to the sound of beautiful, peaceful flute music coming from the other room. Opening the bedroom door, she saw that, just as Michael had said, he had gone, but had left the alarm to wake her with music. She made herself some breakfast and curled up in the cushioned chair to eat it.

Sitting there gave her time to reflect on what she would do now. The longer she stayed, the more chance of her captors finding her. They were probably out looking for her and, because she had broken the rules by getting into a car, and, worse still, not returning, would carry out their threat. She wasn't sure where she was, but she knew that if she did go, she would have to somehow get as far away as possible.

Having made her mind up to leave, she went to find her clothes which she had hung up in the bathroom, but found they were not there. Searching the apartment, she found that they had been cleaned and folded up in a neat pile on one of the dressers in her bedroom, which she hadn't noticed when she woke. On top of the clothes was a note that said:

'I'm away for a while; stay as long as you like. The place is yours. You are safe here – no one will find you. There's food in the cupboards. If you decide to stay, when I get back I will take you home. If you decide not to stay there's a little something in the envelope to help you get away. P.S. Feed my little friend.
God bless,
Michael.'

87

Folding up the note, Jessie smiled. As she opened the envelope a little white feather from the dove floated out into her hand, and then she saw that it contained a large sum of money.

Dressed and ready to leave, she made her way over to the lift, but stopped. The words, 'feed my little friend' came to her. Searching the cupboards, she found the birdseed and filled the gold dish that was there on the balcony. As she made her way back to the lift, the little dove returned to feed on the food she had just put out. The doors opened and, as she stepped in, something inside said to her, "Stay." But her impulsive nature dismissed it. She pushed the button and the doors closed as she watched the white dove feed.

She felt she could relax as she sat on the train, knowing **they** would not find her. The further the train took her, the safer she felt. The hours passed as she stared out of the window. Thinking about the scene of the white dove feeding made her put her hand into her pocket for the feather, but realised that she had left it back at the apartment. She began to consider whether she could muster up enough courage to phone her parents. But her reasoning told her that it was all her fault and that they had probably stopped thinking about her. She had often thought about what she might say if she ever had a chance of phoning them. She decided to get off the train at whatever the next stop was called. Unknown to her, it was the last stop on that line.

Stepping off the train, she could see that she was the only one who had got off. She noticed the only other person there was an old, white-haired man with a porter's hat on, sweeping the platform. As she walked to the exit, the old man said to her, "Nice day!"

"Yes, it is,' said Jessie walking past him. She stopped to turn around and ask, "Is it far to town?"

"About a 40 minute walk," the old man replied.

Because it had been a nice warm day, she had already decided to walk and now knew that she could make it there before dark.

The old man gave her directions, saying, "Take the left fork up the lane."

"How far is the fork?" she asked.

The old man, with a look of concern on his face, said, "I'll tell you what, I'll walk with you and show you the way in case you get lost. I'm all done here."

"Thank you, but I don't need any help. I can find my way," she replied.

"Are you sure you don't need my help there, Missy? Could be a storm brewing!" he said.

Jessie looked up and saw nothing but blue sky and sunshine. "I'm sure," she replied and set off determinedly.

Her clothes weren't really suitable for walking, especially the high heels she was wearing but, because of the circumstances, they were all she had. After a while her feet were blistered and ached so much that she decided to take off her shoes and carry them. After a few steps walking on the gritty road though, her feet felt as if she was treading on hot needles and she had no idea how much further she had to go. Each step was agony and she couldn't imagine how she'd manage to walk the whole distance. The light was fading, and a new worry tried to grow in her mind. She tried to reassure herself: *This is nothing compared to what I've experienced and the plus side is: I am free!*

Her thoughts were interrupted by a voice saying, "You look lost."

It was from a car that had drawn up quietly behind her. She had met many men in the time of her captivity, and the sound of the man's voice didn't make her jump. His face looked concerned, as if he wanted to help.

"I'm trying to find my way to the town," she said.

"You're a long way off! It will be dark before you can get there on foot, especially with no shoes on! That's where I'm heading – I can give you a lift if you like?"

Jessie knew she shouldn't get in the car, but then she knew it wouldn't be good to be out here alone in the dark either. And how she longed to give her sore and painful feet a rest! Trusting in the man's friendly face, she got into the car.

It wasn't long before she noticed that his eyes kept looking down at her legs. She was very conscious of the shortness of her dress, which revealed even more of her legs as she sat in the car. Working on the street, the skimpiness was designed to attract the men.

"What brings you out here?" said the man.

"I've been living in the city and decided to have a trip out for a weekend in the country." It was the first thing that came into her head. How could she tell a complete stranger what she had been up to?

"What's a pretty girl like you doing on your own?"

Jessie laughed a little nervously.

"I'm Stan. What do they call you?"

"Jessie."

"Just Jessie?" he asked.

"Jessie Bell," she replied.

Trying to be funny, he said: "That has a nice ring to it, Jezebel!"

She had to think for a moment about what he meant by calling her that. Then she remembered the name was in the Bible. "No!" she laughed nervously again. Then she thought he wasn't far wrong considering the life she had led.

After what seemed quite a distance, she began thinking to herself: *I didn't think the town was this far*, and she remembered the old man saying, "It's within walking distance." *Maybe he meant using the shortcut, and that's why it seems a long way.* "How much further is the town?" Jessie asked.

"Not far now."

A few minutes later Jessie noticed that they went past a sign pointing left which said that it was two miles to the town.

"Shouldn't we have turned left back there at that sign?"

"No, that's the long way to town. I know these lanes, and this way is quicker."

Jessie assumed he was right and relaxed a little. However that didn't last for long.

The daylight was almost gone and, as it was some thirty minutes since the signpost, she began to have concerns about the man and where he was taking her. "Where are we going?" said Jessie.

"Just a little further," he replied smoothly.

As they came around a corner, the car pulled off the lane into a track in the woods. Jessie's fear was realised and her stomach turned over in panic. She quickly got out of the car to run, but was soon caught up by the man and overpowered as he pulled her to the ground. She screamed and tried to kick him as he dragged her further into the woods. Before passing out, as the attack was going on, she was aware of the sound of crows cawing above as if they were applauding at what was going on.

A large crack of thunder made her come to. She heard the car drive away. Not only had he brutally attacked and abused her, he had taken all her money. After lying there for some time in pain and distress, she managed to get up slowly. Feeling weak and shaken, she started to make her way back to the lane. She stopped short as she heard the sound of a car engine idling. *Could it be her attacker?* In her traumatised state, she was so frightened of the man that she turned back into the woods.

As she made her way deeper in, lightning and thunder filled the air and she could feel the temperature had started to drop, causing mist to come up from the ground. Although in fear of what lay ahead, she had to put as much distance as possible between her and where she was attacked, so she hurried on along the track deep into the woods.

It wasn't long before she had to sit down. Seeing a clearing a little way off the track, she found a tree stump to sit on. Her face and body were hurting from the beating and, with her head in her hands, she wept in despair. She cried out in anguish: "Why, God, why? If you are such a loving God, why did you let this happen to me? Why didn't you stop it?" Her mother's words came to her, telling her that God was a loving God. How she longed to have her mother's arms around her to comfort her, but she was on her own. And what made it worse was the thought of the offer to stay at Michael's apartment that she had foolishly declined, as she might have been home by now.

Still with her head buried in her hands, she could feel her body begin to have the effects of withdrawal symptoms from the drugs that her captives gave her. She recognised the symptoms, as sometimes they would deliberately withhold them. It was their way of making her dependent on them. Strangely, while she was with Michael her body seemed not to need them. But now she had started to feel an overwhelming sense of anxiety, she had started to sweat and she could feel her heart rate increase. Then she felt a chill run through her body, but that was one more effect of the withdrawal.

Something made her look up. She hadn't noticed the big, blackened tree opposite her. She couldn't make out how, but she could see a strange, luminous mist rolling down from the top of the tree. As it reached the ground, it turned into a dark, dense, freezing fog, which rolled outwards, covering the area and settling around her. She didn't know if she was hallucinating or if what she was seeing was real. She knew she had to keep going in case her attacker came looking for her, and also because she didn't know how dense the fog would get. With that and the increasing darkness, it would be easy to get even more lost than she was already.

As a young child, she had got separated from her parents at a very large county show. Her parents were watching the show jumping and nearby farmers were showing their animals. The bleating of the young lambs made her ask her parents if she could go and see them. As it was only a short distance behind them, they agreed but told her not to go anywhere else. Captivated by the lambs, she could see a young calf and many more animals in the pens in the next section, and wandered away from where she was told to stay. Her parents had, every now and then, been turning around to see if she was okay and they were shocked and dismayed when they turned and discovered she wasn't there. The air was filled with the sound of frantic calls of: "Jessie!"

She was oblivious to the commotion as she was in a world of her own, charmed by the young animals. She was suddenly aware of people shouting, then realised that she couldn't see where her parents were and was overcome with fear and panic.

"Mummy! Daddy!" she wailed. "Where are you?"

From behind, a hand gripped her shoulder and she heard: "Don't **ever** do that to us again!"

She was about to pull herself up, when she heard muffled voices in the direction she had just come from. If that wasn't frightening enough, she saw the beam of a torchlight flashing from side to side amongst the trees.

She tried to calm herself by thinking that it might be poachers looking for game.

Then her biggest fear materialized. She heard a voice say: "She's out here somewhere! She couldn't have got far."

So now there were two of them! Her throat tightened with fear.

She heard them laughing, and calling out: "Jezebel, where are you? Where are you, Baby? We **will** find you, Sweetheart!"

In her childhood she had played the game 'hide and seek' with her friends and it had been exciting, but these men were not her friends and it was no game. It was real and she was terrified!

Panic-stricken, she quickly hid herself behind the big tree, hoping that the fog would hide her from them. Her hopes turned to dismay as the fog started to clear from where she was hiding, yet was still dense elsewhere. It was as if the fog was on their side and showing them where she was. Now she knew it wouldn't be long before they'd find her.

She noticed that nearby was a big dead tree that was hollowed out. It was big enough for her to squeeze into and hide so she wedged herself into the dark, damp cavity and waited, stifling a scream as something light and furry crawled over her. Too scared to make a sound or run, she could hear her heart racing with a loud beat. Under her breath, she pleaded, "Jesus, please help me!" When she was a child her mother had told her that if she had a problem or was in trouble that she should call out to Jesus.

The light of the torch was now shining her way. If it hadn't been for the hollow tree where she was hiding, she knew they would have seen her. Still frozen, she could see one of the men as he stood with his back only inches away from her, shining his torch the other way. She could even smell his cheap, strong aftershave - which she had already smelt in the car - and it made her feel sick. The fact that he didn't hear her heart beating was a miracle! But her miracle was to be short lived.

On the ground, between her and the back of the man, appeared a large black crow, which started cawing at her. The noise of the crow made him start to turn around and her heart stopped in fear at what was about to happen to her.

With her eyes tightly closed, she heard the other man say: "Quick! Someone's coming!" and they ran back from where they had come, disappearing into the fog.

Not knowing who the 'someone' was, she stayed put, still too frozen in fear to move from inside the tree. Slowly she turned her head in the direction that the 'some body' was coming from. Again she said, "Jesus, if you are there I need you now!" She could see a dim light further in the woods, coming her way through the fog. She desperately wanted help, but this could be another person coming along to hurt her. She closed her eyes and decided to stay where she was and wait, hoping whoever it was would pass by.

She could hear the twigs and leaves being disturbed as whoever it was came closer. Then, adding to her terror, she heard a noise that she had never heard before, a noise of groaning combined with a high pitched screaming wind. Forcing herself to open her eyes, she could see it was the chilled fog being funnelled back into a dark hole that had opened in the ground. Even though her fear stopped her from moving, she could see the light coming along the track. As it approached, each tree ahead of it was lit up and the closer it came, the brighter it shone. Her hopes of it going past disappeared as the light stopped by her tree. Still curled up in the hollow, Jessie held her breath, petrified.

There was a pause, then the silence in the wood was broken by a soft voice saying, "Jessie, you are safe now. There's no need to be frightened anymore. I have come to take care of you."

Jessie was still scared but, because the voice sounded so gentle and reassuring, she slowly peered out from within the tree to see who had spoken. All she could see was a bright, glowing light but it felt as though it was radiating a warm, encompassing love that seemed to penetrate the tree and saturate her.

"Come to me, Jessie, I have provided a friend to take you to safety," the gentle voice said.

Jessie found herself coming out from the protection of the tree and walking towards the light, but stopping a few yards from it.

The reassuring voice said, "Come closer, Jessie, I have heard your cry."

All trace of fear had left her. Her hand reached towards the light, although it was too dazzling to make out anyone. A hand gently held hers and instantly she could feel the withdrawal symptoms of the drugs leave her and a feeling of trust drew her into the light.

To her amazement there was the little white dove on the ground that she had seen at Michael's She began to wonder if she was dreaming. It was all so strange!

"No, Jessie, it's not a dream. I said I would take care of you. Trust me, and hold out your hand."

As she did, the dove flew up, and settled in her hand. A wonderful feeling of peace flooded her being.

"Follow the dove, Jessie."

The dove flew off a little way in front of her to guide her through the wood, and occasionally circled around her. She followed calmly as it led her along the track and again it was as though she was in a pleasant dream.

She was brought out of it by her name being called softly. "Jessie! Jessie, we are here." She found herself standing in front of an old inn.

"Go in, Jessie. In there is what I promised you."

Jessie turned back to face the light and, before she could ask, once more the answer to her question came.

"You have been hurt and experienced terrible things, and you have asked why I didn't help you. I did Jessie. I sent several people to help you and to take you to safety."

Jessie was about to ask, "Whom?"

The voice said, "Michael, and the old man at the station. But you said "No" to their offers of help. I can only help if you say, "Yes", but you chose not to. I was there with you, giving you strength to endure what you went through. When you cried, Jessie, I cried with you. The pain you felt, I felt."

"But I don't get it. Why didn't you stop me from going to the nightclub in the first place? Then none of those things would have happened to me!"

"It was your choice to go there, Jessie. I never control or force people; I always give them freedom to choose. But, because you called out to me, I was able to come to you. I have taken all that part of your life away and made you strong. You can now live your life as it was meant to be. Don't forget, Jessie, I am always with you. If you ever need me just call." And with that the light disappeared into the darkness of the track.

She turned to the doors of the inn, and there on the ground in front of the doors was a little white dove feather. Smiling to herself, she picked it up and held it tightly to her heart as she walked through the doors of the inn.

The first thing she set eyes on was the smiling face of an old, bearded man who looked vaguely familiar.

"Welcome, Jessie! I was told you were coming. Come and take a seat. There are some people I would like you to meet," said the man.

Instantly Jessie remembered what the voice in the light had said about sending someone to help her. *Could this be the man at the station who had offered to walk with her?* She wondered how he knew her name but, after what had just happened, she wasn't totally surprised. She followed him to the table.

"You're in safe hands now, Jessie. I will leave you to introduce yourself."

Esther got up and moved to the next seat so that Jessie could sit down.

"I'm Esther. This is John, and that's Simon and Matthew.

"Jessie," she answered hesitantly, wondering who these people were.

"I know you have lots of questions - but we don't know the answers either," said Esther.

Jessie sat there looking around. She wondered if this could be the long-term effects of some bad batch of drugs that she had been given, or a dream that she was going to wake from any minute, back in the room where she had been held captive.

"What happened to you, Jessie?" asked Esther.

"Happened?" she said, not knowing where to start. Esther sensed, by the look on her face, that she was confused.

"Start from the beginning and tell us how you got here."

Jessie found herself pouring out her story. When she had finished Esther had tears in her eyes. She got up and put her arms around Jessie to comfort her.

Jessie felt a soft hand from behind touch her shoulder. It was the young girl who served in the inn.

"I was told you might need these."

Jessie could see it was a new dress and shoes. She looked over to the barman, who was just smiling at her.

With a look on her face that said "Thank you," she smiled back.

Chapter Six

Lust

Their reactions to Jessie's story were interrupted by the familiar sound of the doors being opened, which made all eyes in the group turn to see who was about to come in. A man entered. He was smartly dressed but hadn't shaved for several days. With a look of bewilderment, he glanced over to where they were sitting.

"Hosea Cohen!" He heard his name being called out, which made him turn to   see an old man with a white beard smiling at him.

"Welcome, Hosea. I was told you were on your way. Come and take a seat."

Slowly he made his way over to the old man, looking slightly on edge.

"Sit down," the old man, said, "Drink this - it will calm you."

Hosea took the drink. After smelling it cautiously, he sipped it. He had never tasted anything like it and he found an instant calmness come over him as he drank it down.

"It's good isn't it? How do you feel now?" asked the old man.

"Good. What was that stuff?"

The old man smiled and said, "It's a very old recipe of my father's. Come with me – there are some people waiting to speak to you." He took him over to the group, who were still looking towards him.

"This is Hosea. I'm sure you've all got something to talk about," he said, chuckling as he made his way back to the bar.

They made room for him at the table, and introduced themselves.

"Sit down here," Esther said. "No questions - just tell us what happened to you out there."

"Come on, Esther, he hasn't even sat down yet. Give him a chance!" John said.

Hosea moved a chair so he could sit down. There was no getting away from the expectant looks on their faces as they sat patiently waiting for him to speak.

"I'm not sure where to start. How far back do you want to hear?"

"Tell us about yourself and then how you got here," John said before Esther had a chance to ask.

Hosea's mind went back to the time when he was lost, the time when he first saw Gomer.

He had found himself wandering in a street, miles away from his normal surroundings. Although he was brought up in a Jewish religious background, he wasn't naive about the area he had wandered into, with the

102

flashing lights and men enticing whoever passed their doorway to see the girls that were inside. As he walked along the street, he was approached by several women, asking him if he wanted to 'do business', but he smiled and walked on by. Then his eyes were drawn to the beauty of a woman dressed in a royal blue, eastern-looking outfit that reminded him of an Indian princess. He could see the bright flashing lights of the street reflecting in her shiny hair. At first she didn't notice him staring at her, but then something made her look in his direction. Hosea felt an attraction, which he couldn't understand. This was a loose woman that he knew he shouldn't be looking at. But what was it that made him continue to stare? There were so many things about her that held him captive. He couldn't make his mind up whether it was her long black hair or her almond-shaped, vivid blue eyes. Then something inside him said, "Take this woman for your wife."

Before he knew what was happening she approached him, saying, "You like?"

"Sorry for staring!" he said, "Yes, I like very much."

"You pay me first, then you have," she said.

"No... Not like that," he said, embarrassed.

"How do you like then?" she said, not understanding - as she wouldn't have had to have a conversation like that with another man.

"It's ... I have never seen such a beautiful woman as you."

For the first time in her life, she felt embarrassed by such words. "What do you want then?" she asked him.

He found himself saying: "Can I pay you just to talk?" She had never been asked before to 'just talk', but said, "You pay me and we talk."

Hosea took out of his wallet a wad of notes. "How much?" She took each note, slowly gauging his reaction as she continued. Hosea could see the amount she was taking, but considered the time he could spend talking to her was worth it.

She took him to a small room above one of the brightly lit doorways of the building she was working from. In the short time he had with her he had found out that her name was Gomer and she had come to his country several years ago. Her parents came from Israel but she was half Indian, as her mother was from India. As the girl of the family, she was encouraged at an early age to use her body as a means of bringing money into the home.

"Where abouts in Israel?" he asked.

"Why do you want to know?"

"It's just that my parents come from Israel."

"A place called 'Ephraim'. Do you know it?" she asked.

"No, I don't know it, although I think I've heard of it. I was born here, but I should think my parents might. They come from a place called Kadesh. I think it's further north than Ephraim."

"So you are Jewish as well?"

"Yes, I think we have something in common. Can I see you again?" he asked.

"Yes - if you pay."

"Yes, I pay," he replied, smiling. "Bye, Gomer."

She fluttered her long eyelashes at him as he closed the door.

After several visits with Hosea not wanting anything but to talk, she could see that he was different than the rest. She had been used to men treating her as an object to be used and not caring about her as a person. It hadn't bothered her before as that was just the way it was. But here was someone who treated her with respect and dignity, as though she mattered. At first she had been sceptical but he gradually gained her confidence, until she was able to think that maybe she could start afresh with such a man, who didn't condemn her for what she was or had been.

It wasn't long before he had persuaded her to leave her sordid life and start a new one with him, as his wife. And so several years passed and she bore him three lovely children. He loved her more each day, as did the children. He thought they couldn't be happier.

But gradually a spirit of discontentment came upon her. She started to say to her husband that she wanted to have a night out with her girlfriend, and then, after a while, one night led on to two and before long she was going out almost every night. Eventually she was making excuses for not coming home some nights. Because of his love for her, he accepted her excuses but, deep down, little thoughts of suspicion were whispering in his ear. Had she gone back to her old way of life?

One night he arranged for a friend to look after the children so that he could follow his wife. He was praying that what he found that night would not be what he feared. Without knowing, she led him to a bar in the street where he had first met her. He hid in the crowd making sure she couldn't see him, but was in a position that he could still see her. To his relief, he saw her girlfriend join her at the bar … but what he saw next made his heart sink. Two men came and sat each side of them. He couldn't hear the conversation but could see it was more informal than polite conversation, as one of the men put his arm around his wife and was whispering something in her ear. Worse, he could see that she was enjoying it and laughing. Then his stomach churned as he watched something happen which he had feared deep down. His wife stood up and took the hand of the man beside her and led him up the stairs.

He went home and sat looking at the clock. As the hours went by, he occasionally got up to look out of the window if he heard a car outside. Patiently he waited, hoping that she would come home that night.

In the early hours he heard a car pull up. He quickly went to the curtains to peer out and saw his wife get out of the vehicle before it drove away. He could hear her fumbling, trying to put the key in the front door, followed by the key turning and the door being opened and quietly closed. She was creeping around so that she wouldn't wake him, obviously hoping that she could sneak into bed without him noticing. But the words, "You're late dear," came from the darkened room. With her high heels in her hands, she turned from the stairs, shocked to see her husband standing behind her. Turning on the light he said, "Did you have a good night with your friend?"

"What are you doing up?" she said surprised.

"I was worried about you and decided to wait up for you."

"Yes, sorry I'm late. I missed my bus and caught the late one."

He knew that was the first lie. It was the first of many to follow. So where did you go tonight then?"

"I went to the cinema with my friend."

"*Lie two*," he said under his breath. "Good film?"

She stumbled for words as she obviously knew he would ask her next which film they'd seen. "Err, it was okay - it was a spur of the moment decision to go, but it was a romance. You know how I like romantic films."

She started to stroke his arm and flutter her long eyelashes at him, probably thinking that he would be distracted and he would stop the interrogation.

He could see what she was trying to do, but this time it wouldn't work. "The truth!" he demanded.

She sat there, avoiding eye contact with him. He knew she was trying to think fast as she didn't know how much he already knew. He sat there patiently looking at her, waiting for an answer.

"The truth is, we did think about going to the cinema, but my friend suggested that we went to a club. I knew you wouldn't have approved so I decided that the cinema story would be better, and thought you would believe me."

"A club! And where was this club?"

"Oh, it was the new one that opened in town. The Jezree."

Hosea knew of it and he knew that she knew he did, and that's why she had said it. But he knew it was just another lie, making it lie number three. He so longed for her to tell him the truth so that he could forgive her. He could live with the act of adultery, even though it hurt. But the lying meant he could never trust her and that hurt even more.

Softly he said to her, "Gomer, you know how much I love you. Can you not tell me the truth?"

"I'm not lying!" she said, raising her voice.

"But you are, Gomer. Do you want to know how I know? I'll tell you! I followed you to that bar," he said bitterly.

There was silence, followed by her crying. "I'm sorry, I'm sorry!" she sobbed.

"Why, Gomer? Wasn't my love enough for you? Did you ever want for anything? Maybe you don't love me, but how could you do it to the children? I just don't understand. Tell me, Gomer, why?"

"It's not you, Hosea. It's me. Ever since you took me away from my street days I have battled with the temptation to go back. You don't know how I've tried! When I looked at you and the children it made the thoughts disappear but, maybe because it's bred in me, they returned and I couldn't stop myself."

"Why didn't you talk to me, Gomer? I could have helped you. I still can – it's not too late.

"Yes it is, Hosea," she said reaching out for his hand. "How can you love a woman like me now?"

"My love is strong enough. It doesn't matter what you have done, I will always love you."

"You say that now, but you will never trust me. It's for the best that I leave. I'm sorry, Hosea, for what I've done to you and the children. I'll leave tonight."

She got up from the table to go upstairs and pack her things. Hosea followed her up the stairs, saying, "It's late! Where could you go to at this time of night? It's not safe out there! If there's nothing I can say to stop you, at least leave in the morning."

He said that, hoping that after a night's sleep she would change her mind.

"Okay, but I want to be gone before the children wake up. I couldn't bear to say goodbye to them."

Hosea didn't get any sleep. He had sat there all night just looking at her asleep, knowing that his beautiful wife would be gone in a few hours.

She awoke to see Hosea standing there with a tray of coffee, toast and a little flower he had picked from the garden.

With a tear running down her cheek, she said, "Don't, Hosea. I haven't changed my mind. Don't make it harder for me than it is."

With that she quickly dressed, packed her bag, and went downstairs. She had one last look around the home. Knowing that he was powerless to stop her, Hosea just stood watching as she went to the front door, but she stopped, turned around and, putting her arms around him, kissed him on the cheek. Hosea held her tight and didn't want to let her go, but she pulled away and left.

Hosea had many sleepless nights, thinking about his wife and where she was. He knew what she was doing but he tried hard not to think about it. One night, whilst lying there, an inner voice said, "Go - show your love to your wife again, though she is an adulteress. Love her, as I have loved her."

Those powerful words lingered with him throughout the day, encouraging him with new hope that he could win her back. He made up his mind; arranged for the children to be looked after by a friend and set off to find her.

The first place he searched was her old haunt, but couldn't see her. He even braved it enough to approach women in their doorways to ask if they had seen her, but that proved unsuccessful. As much as it hurt his feelings remembering the night he saw his wife going upstairs with another man, he went back to the bar but there was no sign of her. He noticed the same barman and asked him if he had seen the woman, Gomer. The man replied, "Yes, she was in here a couple of days ago. All the guys have been coming in, asking for her. She's very popular with the punters!"

Hosea didn't want to hear the last bit, but asked, "Any idea if she's coming in tonight?"

"I don't think so. I heard that she moved on - to Nottingham."

"Any idea where in Nottingham?" Hosea asked.

"No mate, sorry."

After several hours of driving, he arrived in Nottingham and checked in at a hotel. As he hoped, the receptionist was a male.

"I'm new up here. Where's the best place to go to have a little fun around here?" he enquired.

"Depends on what you mean by 'fun'. There's fun and there's fun - if you get what I mean," the man behind the desk replied.

"I mean 'men's fun'," Hosea said.

"Not far. Easy walk, about fifteen minutes up the main street." He named the place. "You can't miss it. It's all happening there!" he said, pointing in the direction with his hand.

"Thanks," Hosea said, discreetly handing him a note from his wallet. Hosea didn't waste any time and set off.

Calls came from several women standing in doorways. He hoped that, just maybe, he would recognise one of those voices as Gomer's. As he walked on, passing girl after girl, he heard the voice he wanted to hear. It was

Gomer's. The shock of seeing him made her smile change to a look of disbelief.

"Hosea, what are you doing here?" was all she could say.

"I came to find you, Gomer. I want you back."

"I can't talk to you. You mustn't be here; it's not safe for you!" she said, glancing to see if the guy she was working for was watching them.

"Why did you come? It only brings pain. Go back, Hosea. I can't go back now – I've moved on. Now, please go."

"I can't. The longing in my heart is too strong for me to forget you. The children miss you! Life's not the same for us, Gomer."

"I'm sorry, Hosea, I can't. I will only hurt you and the children again. You will soon forget me. Anyway, I've met someone else and I don't love you." He knew she was only be unkind to make him leave.

"I don't believe you," he said as he put his hands on her shoulders. "Look me in the eye and tell me you don't love me."

She looked him in the eye and said, "I don't love you. Now go! I don't ever want to see you again. We're all done here".

As Hosea looked into the eyes that once held him captive, he could see that they were the eyes of a stranger; they were cold.

"I just can't let you go. Come with me now," he said as he tried to pull her along the street.

"Let me go!" she cried out, "Go away!"

Her raised voice alerted her minder, who was built like a barn door. He came hurrying over to her.

The minder grabbed Hosea by the arm and swung him around, saying, "Beat it, Bud! Get out of here! The next time I see you bothering one of my girls, it will be the last thing you do!"

Not being a violent man, Hosea looked Gomer in the face and said, "Please!" but she whispered, "Sorry," and turned away.

Hosea knew he couldn't give up on her. He lost himself in the crowded street, but didn't go too far so as to keep her in his sights. He could see the minder had his hands on her shoulders, shouting at her. Everything inside him wanted to go and confront him, but he could see he was no match for someone so big.

Hosea realised that Gomer would probably move on again now that he had found her. He knew she cared about him enough to be concerned that her minder would harm him if he approached her again but he knew she didn't care enough to come back to him. Yet he couldn't let her go without trying once more.

He followed her back to where she was staying, and watched the door all night. In the early hours of the morning, cold and crouched down in a doorway not far away, he heard a door close, which brought him out of his light sleep. It was Gomer. He watched her as she cautiously looked up and down the street to see if anyone was watching then, seeing that it was deserted, she hastily made her way up the street with a small case in her hand. Hosea followed, keeping his distance. He followed her to a taxi rank, where she spoke to a driver through the car window, got in and drove off. He knew that if he went back to get his car he would lose her. He quickly went to the taxi that was waiting behind and got in.

"Where to?" came the voice of the driver.

"Follow that taxi."

"After all the years of driving, that's the first time I've heard those words!" said the driver.

"Don't get too close," Hosea said.

Enthusiastically, the driver sped off in pursuit but kept a discrete distance behind.

Her taxi led him out of the city into the country, finally stopping at a village, where she booked in at a B&B.

Instructed by Hosea, his taxi stopped a safe distance back. After paying the driver, he booked in at the village inn opposite the B&B. His room had a view out the front, which enabled him to keep an eye on the front door of the B&B. He knew that Gomer wasn't an early riser, which gave him the opportunity to recoup some sleep, which he desperately needed.

He was up early and pulled up a chair by the window. After several hours of waiting, he finally saw her leave with her case; she was making her way out of the village on foot. He hurried down to the street and followed her. He realised that, once out onto the country lanes, it would be hard to follow without her seeing him. Once or twice he had to step into the hedgerow as she had stopped, as though sensing that there was someone behind. He could see, by the quickening of her steps, that she realised that she was being followed, then she disappeared out of his sight as she went round a bend in the lane. Hosea increased his pace. He came around the bend to find that the lane before him was completely straight. She was nowhere to be seen. *Where had she gone*? Looking around, he could see a track that led into a wood.

That's the only way she could have gone, he thought to himself.

Stepping into the wood, Hosea could see that it was a dense, dark place and that she would have many places to hide - with good reason, as she didn't know it was Hosea following her.

Maybe she's scared and hiding somewhere, too afraid to move. The thought that he had caused her fear gave him great concern. He knew it was time now to reveal himself. "Gomer! It's me, Hosea. You can come out!" he called.

There was no reply; only the sound of crows cawing after being disturbed. He made his way further into the wood, calling her name; but again there was only silence, apart from the sound of many crows flapping their wings. The distant sound of someone running through the dry, dead foliage made him stop and listen. He was sure he could hear Gomer's voice crying out, "No! .... Go away!" Then it went quiet. The woodland was so dense that he couldn't fathom out which direction the voice had come from. The only thing he did know was that it wasn't from behind him, so he quickly made his way along the track.

Hosea came to a stop; he could see Gomer some distance ahead. She looked exhausted and was trying to get her breath back. As much as he wanted to go to her, he decided to stay in the shadow of the trees, so he could keep an eye on her. Then he heard the familiar words, "How much?"

He saw her turn and behind her had appeared a man with money in his hand. "How much?" the man said again. Gomer gasped, "So, I was right! I *was* being followed!"

As she turned from him, more men appeared all around her saying, "How much? How much?"

"Where are you all coming from?" she cried. This was nothing new but something about these men wasn't right, and he could see that fear had begun to grip her. She ran into the woods but the men were following close behind, calling "How much? How much, Gomer?"

She kept running, with Hosea behind her keeping his distance. He could see she was trying to find the track that would lead her out of the woods, but she tripped on a root and fell face down to the ground. As she turned to get up, there surrounding her, were the men. They were standing over her, reaching out to take her arms. "No!" she cried out, "No!"

As she shrank back, someone called out her name, and it wasn't Hosea! The men retreated from her into the cover of the trees, and Hosea could see that in front of her was a kind of pillar of blue fire with the misty figure of a man in a glowing white robe inside.

"Gomer," the figure said, "There are two paths before each person: a broad path that leads to sin and destruction, and a narrow path that leads to life. You have chosen the broad path and what is happening to you is the repercussion of that choice. But it's not too late. Accept me into your life, and I will free you from it, to go back to your loving husband and children. Choose, Gomer, between me, and what is waiting for you."

Hosea could see the figure in white reaching out his hand and offering it to her.

She hesitated for a long moment and Hosea held his breath. Then she looked back and saw the men standing there with their arms reaching out to her. "Come with us, Gomer! This is the only life you know and enjoy. Come with us!"

She turned back to the man in the white robe, to see his hand still being offered to her but she shook her head slowly. Taking the hands of the men she went away into the darkness of the woods.

"Gomer!" Hosea called desperately. He had almost reached her, but something held him back when he saw what was going on.

When he saw her going off with the men he tried to run after her, but his steps were halted by a figure. It was the same one that had talked to Gomer and given her the choice to make.

"Why do you look for her? She has gone," the stranger said.

"Where? Tell me please!"

"Hosea, she has gone to a place where there is no coming back from - a great divide separates that place from here. She has sowed the wind and reaped the whirlwind."

"I don't understand. Where is this place? I need to find her!" Hosea said with desperation in his voice.

"The only way you can go there is by rejecting me. I offered her my hand to free her from her way of life but her lustful desires made her choose the hand of darkness. She will never find rest from the demands of men and eventually she will be tormented for eternity. Hosea, if you choose to follow her, there is no coming back. Think about your children, waiting for you at home.

Instantly he could see the faces of his children. His heart longed to be with them but if he went back without his beautiful Gomer he didn't know how he could bear it. But then he felt calmness coming over him and the awesome presence of the man in front of him was sinking in.

"Are you for real?" he found himself asking.

"Yes, I am more real than you know. I have always been. I am the beginning and the end, and I offer you a life that your heart desires: true love. Come, Hosea, you are special to me. I don't want to lose you. Take my hand and I will take you to a place that is away from the evil that is here," he said, offering his hand.

The words of the man penetrated his heart. He reached out to take the hand in front of him, stepping into the pillar of fire. The blue flames swirled around him yet, to his amazement, they were cool.

"Who or what are you?" he asked. "How do you know my name?"

All he heard was, "I am the way, the truth and the life. If you follow me you will have a life that you couldn't imagine."

He asked again, "How do you know my name?"

"I have always known you, Hosea. You are one of my chosen people."

He didn't understand but before he could say any more they came to a halt outside an inn.

"Go inside, Hosea. There you will find friends and the start of a new life."

"What about my beautiful wife?" he asked as the pillar of fire disappeared into the woods.

"You will get over your loss, I promise you," he heard as the words faded into the wood.

He turned back to face the inn and stepped through the door.

Chapter Seven

The Gambler

Sitting on the bar stool and looking at the group, I said, "I couldn't help overhearing the stories of what happened to you all. A similar strange thing has just happened to me."

"Come and join us," said Esther. "Tell us your story."

I made my way over and sat with them. Having heard their accounts, I was not so reluctant to share mine.

"Well, I'm Tom and I was a successful businessman, buying and selling properties. My success had given me and my family, a beautiful house and a lavish lifestyle. After a time the excitement of making money wore off. I looked for some other way to bring back the buzz I used to get on closing a deal. It wasn't long before I found it - in gambling.

My father taught me to play cards as a youngster and I was soon going wherever there was a friendly game. As I grew into my teens, it wasn't long before I was playing

118

for real money and high stakes. Cards took over my life until I met my future wife. Then I had a dilemma. Because she hated gambling, she gave me the choice: gambling or her. I chose her and put gambling behind me.

I found that I could apply some of the skills I'd learnt to buying and selling properties, and I soon discovered that I could make more money at it than with gambling; plus it involved less risk, which pleased my wife.

But then I got complacent. Making money had become easy and I needed the thrill of facing a challenge so I found myself again seeking out any card games in the area. This time the stakes were higher. I had all the money I needed to play and win.

As I hadn't played for a long time, I found I wasn't as good as I used to be. I was losing more often, but it didn't worry me as I still had plenty of money to keep playing. The problem was, the more I lost, the more I felt the urge to spend time trying to win back the money. I began neglecting my business and, worst of all, my family.

My money was running out fast. My wife must have noticed a change in me. Not only was I starting to lie about working late or having to work away, but I'd sometimes be up in the middle of the night pacing up and down. I'd never in the past put making money before my family and I had always been a sound sleeper. But gambling seemed to have taken over my will, and I felt as though I had no control.

One day when I'd left early for work a letter arrived, addressed to my wife and me. My wife opened the letter and was shocked to find it was from the bank, informing us that we had exceeded our overdraft. As far as she was concerned, we didn't have an overdraft facility. Even if we did, she thought, we would never have to use it, as there was a small fortune in our account. She was immediately on to the bank to inform them of their mistake, only to be told that there was no mistake and that there had been excessive amounts of money drawn from the account over a short period.

When I came home late that night she was waiting for me. As soon as I walked in, I knew by the look on her face that something was wrong.

"We've had a letter from the bank today saying all the money in our account has gone. How Tom?" she said expecting an answer.

Knowing how she felt about gambling, I tried to think of an excuse. I hadn't realized just how much I had lost at cards.

I told her, "I've been investing money into a new property venture and it's taken more money that I thought - but it wont be long before we'll have all the money back, and more." I hoped the lie had reassured her but I knew I was only buying time.

She asked me if I was all right so I told her I'd had a stressful day and that I needed to get to bed. She said she'd go on up and I told her I was just going to make myself a drink and then I'd follow.

A voice inside piped up: *That's what happens when you lie. At least you told the truth about the day being stressful. Losing that amount of money tonight would make anyone stressed. See what gambling does to you?"*

It's just a setback; I'll win it all back at the weekend. It's the big game.

My wife must have heard me opening and closing drawers. She called out, "Tom! What are you doing down there?"

"Just looking for some papers," I called back, "I'll be up in a minute!"

I found what I had been looking for - the deeds of the house. With the little money I had left, I knew I had one more chance of winning it all back at the weekend. As there was no limit on the stakes, in my madness I decided I would take with me the deeds as a backup. My addiction had such a stronghold on me that I was willing to risk it all, but then, like most gamblers, I felt sure I wouldn't lose.

The weekend arrived and it was make or break. Tension was high at the table. One by one the players left as the stakes were getting higher, till eventually it was down to me and one other. I looked at my hand of cards. It was the best I'd had in a long time and I was convinced I would win.

"Don't do it, Tom! It won't end well."

I shut the inner voice out. I felt that at last my luck had changed. All the money I had was on the table, but it wasn't enough to see the other person's hand. With confidence I put the deeds of the house on the table and called the other player to show his hand. I watched in disbelief as my opponent revealed the winning hand.

I left the game broken, not knowing what to do. I didn't go home for days because I couldn't face my wife to tell her I'd lost all our money and our home. Looking at my phone, I could see I had many missed calls from her, but I didn't have the courage to talk to her.

Using my credit card, I spent several days in a Bed and Breakfast where I was often tormented by the inner voice.

"What happened to 'I know I can', Tom?"

I was so sure I could do it. I don't know what to do now.

"Go home and face the music."

How can I? I've lost it all. She will never forgive me.

"You will never know until you do."

Eventually I found the courage to go home and ask my wife's forgiveness.

When she opened the front door I just stood there, unshaven and with my clothes badly creased, as if I'd been living rough. The minute she saw me, she could tell by the state of me that something was wrong.

I forced myself to admit all that I'd got up to and told her how sorry I was. I told her over and over that I knew what a fool I'd been and that I would never do it again. She just sat there at first - too numb, I guess, to speak. Then she responded by reminding me of the promise I'd made when we first met, that I'd chosen her over gambling. Now I'd broken that promise, she said, she could never trust me again. I sat at the table with my head in my hands, watching as she took the children, leaving me to wallow in regret.

I couldn't stay in the house which wasn't mine any more so I left with just a small bag and my travelling companions, 'Guilt' and 'Conscience', to go wherever life would take me. I stayed for one or two nights with so called 'close friends,' who were soon fed up with me feeling sorry for myself and made it clear that it was time for me to move on.

I had come from the top of the ladder of success to the bottom rung. I had become one of the homeless - living rough like those I'd seen many times on the streets. Instead of being the giver, I became the pitiful receiver.

The regret was so strong that it made me give up on life. At cards I'd made a name for myself: 'Lucky Tom, the Unbeatable', but I came to be known as: 'Tom, the Downbeat'.

Then one night I was lying in the doorway of a boarded-up shop, exhausted from not having much sleep in the cold. I was woken by the words:

"This place looks cosy!"

Standing in front of me was a tall man with long hair and a coat going down to his ankles. I thought he was after my doorway so I told him to go and find his own.

"I don't need your place. I've got many nice places of my own," he told me.

I asked him what he was after then.

He sat down next to me and said, "I'm after nothing. I just thought you would like some company."

I hadn't had that in a long time but I said to him, "It looks as if you've made your mind up, whether I want it or not." But if the truth was to be known, I longed for companionship.

"I take it that's a 'yes' then?" he said.

"Whatever," I grunted back.

"I'm Gabe."

"Tom," I answered a little more civilly.

Gabe took a paper bag from his coat pocket and offered me a sandwich, saying, "Hungry, Tom?"

"Always hungry!" I told him as I took one of the sandwiches. "It's good of you to share with me," I said with my mouth full, eager to cram in more.

"My pleasure, Tom. I know what it's like to be hungry," he said.

I asked him how long he'd been on the streets.

123

"It seems like forever, Tom. I must confess I do get around, but I enjoy it."

"Enjoy it! What's to like about this way of life? If I had another chance it sure would be different," I said.

"You say that like a man with regrets, Tom."

"Regrets? That's all I do have," I told him.

"What happened, Tom?" he asked me.

Because I had relived it all so many times, I just said, "If you've been on the streets as long as you say, you've probably heard it all before."

"Well then, Tom", he said, "I'll tell you what I tell all the others. You may be down now, but you don't have to be out. Never give up hoping. If your heart is sincere about finding forgiveness, or whatever it is you need to get you back, it will happen. You've got to want it enough. It's the same hunger as an addiction - where you cannot stop and it drives you on until it happens."

It's strange that he should use the word: 'addiction', I thought to myself, having experienced how strong an addiction can be. "How come you're still here then?" I asked him.

"It's become my way of life - so much so that I consider it a job."

"What, your job is to help people be more positive?" I said.

"Try to, Tom. Some people listen and get their lives back, but other's don't and are content to dwell in their pity parties, spending the rest of their lives in misery."

"If only life could be that easy!" I answered.

"I am sure, Tom, that you can do it. You're one of those who want to have their life back as it used to be, aren't you?" he asked.

"What wouldn't I give for that to happen!" I told him. Looking back to the peaks in my life, I realised I **could** do it. In fact, I had bought many a run-down place and restored it, selling it for a huge profit. Gabe's words of encouragement seemed to rekindle a fire in me that had gone out.

"Are you a God-fearing man, Tom?" he asked me.

"Not really, I told him. "When I was young, I did get drawn into a convincing debate about God by someone on the street, but when I got home and discussed it with my father, he put his point of view over and said, "You don't want to get involved in all that stuff." I've had doubts about the subject ever since."

Then he said: "What would it take, Tom, for you to be convinced that the person on the street was right?"

"Being given my life back! If there is a God, and he's supposed to be kind and all that stuff that the person said, how come I'm here like this, living rough and hungry?" I challenged.

"He didn't make that happen, Tom. You did."

"That's right! Blame me! That's just a cop out of an answer!" I was beginning to get angry.

"Can you honestly tell me, Tom, that before you did anything that you knew wasn't right, you didn't feel a check from inside you about doing it?"

I knew he was right, but I replied, "Look, Gabe. I don't mean any disrespect, but I don't need any preacher pushing religion down my throat. I've got enough on my plate."

"You're right, Tom, about religion," he said, "but wrong about me being a preacher. Religion - you don't need, but you do need help getting your life back on track, and there is someone who can do that for you."

"Who's that then?" I asked, puzzled.

"Jesus. Just asked him to take control of your life, Tom, and He will help you."

"You're doing your preacher bit again, Gabe," I told him.

"I'm not a preacher, Tom."

"Then what are you?"

"More of a messenger."

"I know you mean well, Gabe," I said, "and I'm sorry if I sound ungrateful by the way I'm talking, but living rough and being hungry all the time has made me angry with life. I told you I don't want religion and you offer me Jesus! Now tell me the difference!

"Religion is a set of rules made by men that will tie you down, but Jesus can set you free," he answered.

"How?"

"Just ask him."

I was getting sleepy and could hardly keep my eyes open. Gabe didn't say anymore but just sat down beside me until I was asleep.

When I woke the next morning from a sound sleep I was surprised at how warm I felt, which was unusual as I could see by the frost that the night had been very cold. Looking down, I could see the reason for the warmth. It was Gabe's large, heavy coat that had been laid over me. I stood up to try it on and was amazed that it fitted me. It was as if it was tailor-made for me, and it was of fine quality. When I put my hands in the pockets to keep them warm, I could feel a paper bag in each one. I took them out and looked in them, to see that Gabe had left another sandwich for me in one, and in the other was a little money.

I set off, not knowing where my journey would take me, but with rekindled fire and optimism. I knew somehow that things would work out for me after the hope and encouragement Gabe had put in my heart. I knew it was time to move on and stop feeling sorry for myself.

I travelled from town to town, village to village, wherever I could find odd jobs to earn enough money to keep my hunger at bay. I preferred the rural areas as the solitude of the quiet lanes gave me peace to think about how to go forward with my life.

One day I was making my way out of a village, when I saw a down-and-out like myself sitting on the verge. I made eye contact with him and said, "All right mate?" as I walked by.

"Yea, don't suppose you got anything to eat?" he called to me.

I didn't want to stop but, knowing what it felt like to be hungry, I couldn't just keep walking. The only food I had was half a sandwich that I was saving for later. I turned back and gave it to him.

As he ate the sandwich he said to me, "I've seen you back there at the village - a couple of nights ago."

"How do you know it was me?" I asked him.

"There's not many on the streets who have a warm coat like that," he answered.

"I sat down alongside him and said "I'm Tom."

"Pete," he replied.

I asked him where he was heading.

"Anywhere life takes me," he said. "And you?"

"The same," I told him.

"Mind if I tag along?" he asked.

"Why not? To be honest, I could do with the company. Okay then, we'd better get on our way - if we're going to make the next town or village before it gets dark."

As we set off along the lane, I asked Pete how long he'd been on the streets.

"Since I left the army," he said. "I couldn't adjust to civilian life and, with no job, here I am."

"That's tough," I sympathised. "Did see much action?"

"Plenty. Mostly overseas - you see more than you want to see, stuff that you can't forget. The drink helps," he said, offering me a swig from the bottle he was carrying.

"No thanks," I said, "sounds as if you need it more than me."

As we were talking, we came to a sharp bend. On the right of the bend I could see a track leading into the woods. I don't know what it was about that track but it made me stop. For some reason, I felt tempted to go along it.

"What you stopping for?" Pete asked as he walked further along.

I peered down the track but decided to give it a miss and went on to catch Pete up. Without warning the heavens opened! There was a loud crack of thunder, pelting rain and the noise of what sounded like hundreds of birds flapping their wings and calling out. We both turned around and ran back to the track to take cover.

Sheltering under the trees waiting for the rain to stop, again I could feel an overwhelming curiosity to see where the track went.

"Where do you reckon the track goes to Pete?' I said, not really expecting him to know.

"Not sure - it could lead anywhere," he answered, "but I reckon if we don't want to spend the night in the woods, we should keep to the lane - in spite of the rain. There's got to be a village not far."

We were soon on the lane again but there was something about the track that made me turn around and go back to it. Again I found myself standing there at the entrance and again I could feel there was something tugging at my curiosity; I had a strange desire to follow the track. Not able to resist any longer, I entered the woods.

"You're not listening, Tom! You'll get lost in there!" Pete called out.

I could see the daylight only penetrated a little way in before it was almost lost in the dark, dense foliage. The tranquillity of the woods gave me an idea - of making a shelter to stay in. The semi-darkness suited me, and it would be hard for any walkers passing through to see that anyone was living there - making it an ideal place.

By then, Pete (slightly annoyed) had followed me.

"Hey, Pete," I said, "I've got an idea! What about making a shelter in here?"

Pete had apparently spent many a night in a makeshift shelter in a forest whilst fighting, and would be used to it.

Making our way deep into the woods, Pete was drawn to a tree that was bigger than all the others. Although the light there wasn't very good, he could still see that the large branches of the dark leaf canopy spread wide and would give us protection from any rain and would be safer and warmer than the shop doorways of the towns.

"What do you reckon, Tom? Under this tree would be a good place!" I agreed with him and it wasn't long before we had a shelter made of branches and bracken leaves under the tree.

Apart from the fact that I was always cold, I was content with this way of life to start with. But it gave me plenty of time to think about how I came to be there, which began to cause a deep heaviness to come upon me – undoing the positive outlook my encounter with Gabe had given me. The long, lonely nights being away from my family sent me back into deeper depression. I hadn't realised that the dark atmosphere of the woods was slowly affecting my mind. Pete's screaming in the night, reliving his time in action, only added to the depressive atmosphere.

My only relief came when it was my turn to go back into the village to search for any out-of-date food from the shop bins. But when it was my turn to stay behind, I would sit on a log outside the shelter, tormenting myself over the mistakes that led to my downfall. My only company came from the crows that were somewhere in the tree above, constantly cawing as if they were communicating with each other.

One night we were sitting on our logs, staring into the small fire Pete had made, when I broke the silence and said, "Is it me, or is the wood brighter than usual tonight?"

Pete looked up, "Yea, you're right."

The light of a full moon occasionally broke though the canopy of trees, but it was the dappled effect of the light on the ground that drew my attention. Fascinated by the swirling shapes, I could see that the mottled shapes that I thought were leaves were now turning into the shapes of birds.

"Are you am seeing what I'm seeing Pete?" I asked.

"Seeing what, Tom?" he said in a sleepy voice, disturbed from drifting off.

"Those leaves are turning into birds!" I gasped.

With heavy eyes, Pete looked down. "Na, they're leaves, mate. You need some sleep."

Mesmerised by the shapes, I had an uneasy feeling that something was looking down at me from the trees above. Hesitantly, I looked up and found I was looking at hundreds of small pairs of red, piercing eyes; then I realised they were the eyes of black crows peering down at me. It made the hairs on the back of my neck stand up, I can tell you!

"Pete!" I whispered, "Pete!"

But Pete wasn't listening. He was fast asleep.

I was still looking up at the crows, when suddenly I caught something disturbing out of the corner of my eye. I thought I saw a dark figure slip past me into the cover of the trees, but when I quickly turned my head there was nothing unusual. Just as I convinced myself that it was only my imagination, to the other side I saw another black figure dart past me. I could feel the air temperature was rapidly falling, chilling me to the bone, so I decided to retire to the shelter.

"Pete!" I said, shaking his shoulder. "The temperature's dropping. We'd better get inside." Although it was cold in there, I knew it would be a little warmer than it was outside. Still half asleep and with a grunt, he crawled in and went straight back into a deep sleep. I almost envied him, not for the life he had experienced in the army, but being able to sleep. Lying there trying to fight off the cold, hunger, and tormenting thoughts, it was impossible for me even to doze.

The silence was broken by the sound of something outside, not far from the shelter; the sound of twigs and undergrowth breaking - as if something big was approaching. Whatever it was, it had stopped outside.

"Pete! There's something outside!" I said, poking him hard.

"What now?" he said crossly.

"I heard something outside, listen!"

Pete crawled to the entrance of the shelter.

"What're you doing?" I said, alarmed, "You don't know what's out there."

"Whatever it is, it can't worse than I experienced in a war zone, not knowing where the next shot would come from. I'm not afraid of anything!" And with that he went outside to face whatever it was.

I stayed where I was, listening for the sound of Pete's voice. But I heard only silence.

"Pete! Pete!" I whispered. "You there?"

Still there was no answer. Suddenly there was a piercing scream and Pete's voice shouting, "Get away! Get away!" It filled the woods and quickly faded into the depths.

Too scared to worry about what had happened to Pete, I could only think about myself. I held my breath and didn't dare move. There was silence. Had whatever it was been satisfied with taking Pete and gone? Or did it know that there was someone else inside the shelter? My throat was so dry I desperately needed to cough but I clamped my hand over my mouth.

About to explode, I could hold back no longer. At that moment, a heavy breathing and groaning, like nothing I had ever heard before, told me that whatever was outside wasn't human. I didn't move, hoping that whatever was making the sound would go on by. I could feel the cold intensifying so much that the walls and roof inside the shelter had started to cover in ice crystals and my breath turned into a white vapour. With every breath I took, the icy air felt as though it was freezing my lungs. My teeth started to chatter and every fibre of my being was shaking with the cold. If it wasn't for the warm, heavy coat that Gabe had given me, and the little warmth of my lighter, I knew I would soon freeze to death.

My mind went back to a scene, set in the woods, from a horror film that I once saw when I was young and my imagination started conjuring all sorts of nightmare thoughts. A high-pitched, whistling wind that seemed to be calling my name suddenly filled the air and the flame of my lighter blew out. I began to think I was reliving a scene from the film, which must have imprinted on my mind, as there was no other explanation for it.

Just as I thought it couldn't get any scarier, from the sides and under the bit of sacking that we had as a door, I could see smoky fog creeping in and filling the shelter. My imagination was running wild, I thought. Nothing could have prepared me for what I was to see next. The fog was taking on the form of two clawing hands coming towards me. I pushed myself back into the branches of the shelter and put my arms over my face to protect myself.

After what seemed like ages in that position, I felt nothing. I slowly brought my arms down - to see the fog receding under the sackcloth door. I could sense that the evil presence that had come with the fog was gone, and I could also feel the temperature of the air was returning to normal. Plucking up courage, I made my way outside to see what was going on.

133

Everything seemed to be normal.   Again I tried to figure out if what I had just experienced was real or not. Then I decided that it had to be real as Pete had experienced it as well, unless Pete had been a part of my imagination too. Then it came to me: it could be the effect of what I had thought were mushrooms, that I had picked earlier from the woods and had eaten. I concluded that they must have made me hallucinate.

Thinking that it was all over, my attention was drawn to a small glowing light that seemed to be weaving in and out of the trees. It appeared to be coming towards me from the darkest depth of the wood and it certainly brought me out of my confused state. Before I had a chance to see clearly what the light was, I heard a voice that seemed to come from all around me.

"Thomas, these dead leaves all around you had to die so that new leaves can live.   If you let your old ways die you too can start a new life."

I stepped backwards and tripped over a log. As I got to my feet, I could see the figure of a man with an aura of light radiating around him. I just stood there, not knowing what to think, but there was something about him that made me feel unafraid.

My thoughts were broken by the voice again, saying: "Thomas I have come to help you and break the chains of addiction from you, so you can live again, free from it."

I'd never experienced anything like this before, so to test the reality of the situation, I decided to ask a question but, before I could, the voice said, "Thomas, I knew your name before you were born."

He had answered the very question I was going to ask!

The voice went on: "Thomas, I know everything about you - your past and your future."

This time I managed to speak. "Who are you? What do you want of me? Was all that fog stuff you as well?"

"No, Thomas. There is evil in these woods and the fog is a part of that evil, which had come for you and Peter. I am the true life and, as I have told you, I have come to help you and set you free. Choose, Thomas, life or death."

I thought to myself: *What does that mean choose life or death*? "Do you know what happened to Pete?" I asked.

"Yes, I found him running in the woods. I tried to help him, as I am with you, by asking him to choose between life and death. He had many opportunities to call out to me in his life and, even now with such evil around him, unfortunately he still chose the path that leads to death."

"So where is he now?"

"He holds onto unforgiveness towards the people who killed his comrades, and it has hardened his heart. But more importantly his rejection of me has taken him to a dark place of no return, to be forever tormented."

Then I heard the words: "Your old way of life, Thomas, was leading you to death. I offer you a new way. Life."

"Come, Thomas. Walk with me and I will show you how to live again. Let me take you out of here, to a place of safety. Take my hand."

Thoughts were racing through my mind. Those words 'live again' – that was all I wanted to do, to be forgiven for what I had done to my family, for things to go back as they were before I'd messed up so badly.

As though in a dream, I found myself saying, "Life!" and taking his hand.

As we walked along the track, I could see he was taking me further than I had ever ventured before. I could sense that, each side of the track was a dark presence that seemed unable to come any nearer, and somehow I felt safe.

While walking with him time seemed to have stood still, for it seemed only seconds had passed from when I took his hand and then I heard him say:

"Here's where you find the start of your way home, Thomas. Don't forget: the *love* of money is the root of all evil."

I was trying to think where I had heard those words before, and also there was something strangely familiar about him that I couldn't place, but then my thoughts were distracted by the sound of laughter and singing. I noticed it was coming from an inn, set back from the track and I was drawn towards it. I stopped at the door and, as I turned around, I saw the man walking away.

I called out, "Who are you? How do you know me?"

"I have always known you, Thomas; I am the voice in your heart, gently telling you what to do or not to do. When you gave in to the temptation of gambling, I was that inner voice saying, "Resist!" but you ignored what you knew was right and succumbed to the temptation, leading you to deep regret. I have many names but now, for you, it is: 'Freedom'. I am always with you. If you ever need me, Thomas, call me."

Before I had a chance to ask any more questions, he disappeared into the darkness, with the words floating back, "Stop doubting, Tom! By the way, how's the coat?"

"Gabe?"

I stood there for a while, with those words echoing through my head. What I had just experienced would have made anyone doubt their sanity, even if they believed in the supernatural. I came on in here and sat on a bar stool until you invited me over, and that's it really."

Having just finished telling my story, I heard the familiar sound of the doors being opened - to see a man come through with the same baffled look on his face that each of us had worn, which told us that he too had a story to tell . . .

Chapter Eight

The Alcoholic

As I came through the doors, I stood there for a while looking around. I could see a group of people staring at me, which made me wonder if there was something unusual about me. As I continued to stand there, a strange sensation came upon me that I had never experienced before. I found myself muttering the words, "Welcome, Philip, we've been expecting you," and I knew somehow that these words would be coming from the old, white-haired man behind the bar. To my astonishment, those exact words were then spoken by the old man! I was thinking, *That's uncanny! How did I know that?* Then he said, "Take a seat, Philip," so I made my way over to sit at the bar. The old man produced a strange concoction, the colour of which I had never seen before so, before drinking, I raised it to my nose to smell it. I was surprised that a drink could smell of so many different aromas; it took me back to my childhood days of sodas and colas with lots of choices of flavours. The drink had one more surprise: as I swallowed a mouthful, I could instantly feel a sobering effect come upon me. I sat there for a while, then, finishing my drink, I found myself muttering the words: "There are some people I know you would like to meet." Again, I knew they were the next words the old barman would say . . . which was confirmed a few minutes later when I heard the same words come from the old chap's mouth!

Then, if that wasn't bizarre enough, a picture suddenly appeared in my mind - it was of the old man going to a table behind me to the group of people that were staring at me when I came in. Although I hadn't really paid attention to them, I knew that there were seven people sitting there, two women and five men.

I even knew their names, which I said under my breath: "John, Esther, Simon, Matthew, Jessie, Hosea and Tom." I also knew that Esther was going to invite me to sit with them and I couldn't help thinking: *Considering Esther was a shy, withdrawn person, she is certainly filled with boldness now.* My next thought was: *How did I know that? I've only just seen her!* It was so strange – as though I was reading the script of a book, but how could that be? I had to pinch my arm to see if I could feel it. I could, so I decided I wasn't dreaming.

I turned around slowly to see the old man talking to Esther, then glancing back at me and smiling as all the others turned their eyes in my direction. The old chap made his way back to the bar and said, "There are some people I know you would like to meet."

As I looked over to the table, Esther called out, "Philip, come over here and tell us your story!"

"Yes, we want to hear it," said John.

I made my way over, already knowing what I would do and say next. They all moved up a seat so that I could sit down.

"Sit next to me!" Esther said.

They sat there with a look of expectation on their faces.

"Philip, . . . your story," Esther prompted.

I heard myself say: "I don't really have a story to tell. One minute I was in front of my computer, then I found myself in the woods, drunk, and experiencing a bright light surrounding me, and then hearing a voice telling me to get on the back of . . ."

"A tandem?" interrupted Esther.

"I was going to say 'a bike', but yes a tandem."

"Then what happened?" she asked.

"The last thing I remembered was sitting in my office, as I said. Then a foggy darkness came over me and when it cleared I found myself with a wine bottle in my hand, staggering through a misty, dark wood. Even though I was under the influence of alcohol, I could sense something sinister in the wood. Over and over in my mind, I could hear the words: "Don't leave the track!"

The sudden appearance of two lights coming towards me, made me stop. I could see that one of the lights was towards my left and the other towards my right. As I blinked the lights centralised and merged into one. Then, as if to play tricks on me, they separated into two. Then back into one. I tried to stand still but my body was swaying to and fro, although I still had enough sense to realise that it was the effect of the drink that was making me sway and causing the lights to separate.

The light was coming closer to me, still separating and merging. As I tried stepping to the left to move out of the way, the light went to the left, and then as I went to the right the light also went to the right. Whichever way I went, the light followed me. Then the lights were on top of me.

Still in a drunken state, my mind conjured up the scene of me being a matador and the light being the bull. As the bull came charging towards me, I stood my ground to the last minute and shouted, "Ole!" then quickly threw myself out of the way. I landed to one side of the track, on my back amongst the bracken and leaves.

As I lay there with my eyes closed, I could feel something rapidly crawling over me and could hear a rumbling in the ground beneath me, followed by a sinking sensation that made me open my eyes. As if in some dark nightmare, I could see that I was covered in black ivy and that the ground where I was laying was slowly swallowing me, burying me alive. The more I struggled to stand up, I found the ivy strengthened its pull on me, dragging me back down deeper and deeper into the ground. I sensed that something in the bowels of the ground wanted me. A nightmare vision filled my head: I was the helpless prey of a spider, I was stuck in its web and now the spider was coming for me.

All that was left above the ground were: my head, covered in the black ivy with only my eyes peering out, and one hand that still held on to the bottle. I could feel the pressure of the ground squeezing my eyes from their sockets and the remaining air from my lungs as the ground closed in on me. Gasping for air, I knew that any second I would be gone - buried in the darkness below.

Desperately choking, I heard a voice say, "Philip, let go of the bottle. I cannot help you until you do."

I could hear the words but I couldn't see anyone.

"Let go of the bottle, Philip! It's the power of the drink in the bottle that has control over your will. Until you choose to let go, I cannot save you."

I tried with all my might to let go, but found I couldn't loosen my grip as the ivy had wrapped itself around my hand, holding it tightly to the bottle. It was as if the ivy and the power of the bottle did not want to let go of me. I could feel myself being drawn deeper and deeper down into the dark depths.

As my head went beneath the soil, leaving only the bottle with five fingers grasping it above, a determination that I had never known before came upon me, enabling me to uncoil my fingers from the ivy entangled around the bottle. In the darkness of the earth, I felt a hand reach down and pull me up to the surface.

I found myself standing there – baffled as to how, when I heard a voice say: "Philip! It's time to restore you from being an alcoholic to the successful writer you once were. The dark time that caused you to drink was not my doing. I have come to give you light and set you free from the darkness of addiction."

Thinking that the drink was playing with my mind, I shut and opened my eyes. All I could see was a bright, glowing light all around me and I felt as if I had no control over my body. Still a little dizzy, I could see the silhouettes of two people on bikes in front of me. Confused, I shut my eyes and, when I opened them slowly, I could see only one. The light began to pulsate and a commanding voice said, "Walk this way, Philip."

Having little control over my legs, I was bemused as one by one they started to walk towards the bike, obeying the voice. To my surprise, I realised that my walking was not wobbly but perfectly normal. Then from within the light the voice said, "Get on, Philip."

Again, I found myself obeying.

"Sit back and put your feet up, Philip. I am here to carry you."

As the bike moved off, I couldn't help thinking: *Just as well I feel sober. I would have normally fallen off by now.* Because of my drinking problem, I had been banned from driving and my only means of transport was a bike that I had fallen off many times under the influence of drink.

As hard as I tried, I still couldn't see the person in front clearly as there seemed to be a veil of light between us.

I started to think to myself: *This is all madness! I've got to give up drinking!*

Yet, I still had so many questions to ask, such as: How did the owner of the voice know my name? How did he know that, before the drink, I was a successful writer? And the dark episode in my life - of grief over losing a child, that drove me to drink? As crazy as it seems, even not knowing the answers to my questions, I just sat there, contented to be taken by someone I didn't know to wherever he might decide to take me. I didn't have the slightest idea what was going on!

Engulfed in the light, a great feeling of relaxation came over me, causing my eyes to get heavy and, as hard as I tried to resist, I drifted into a peaceful sleep.

When I awoke I found myself standing outside a familiar building. It was an old inn that I had visualised many times before. I was sure that I knew this place from somewhere but, as hard as I tried to remember, my mind would go blank. It was as if I was dreaming, and yet it was so real.

Somehow, I knew that the next thing I'd hear would be laughter and singing. Instantly, I heard laughter and singing. It was coming from inside the inn. My mind was then filled with a picture of an old, white-bearded man smiling. I felt absolutely certain that, if I went inside, I would see him.

I stepped through the doors to be confronted with the old, white-bearded man behind the bar, smiling.

"And you said you didn't have a story! Is that it?" Esther said.

"Well, there is something else. You may not believe me but the strangest thing is that I know this place and I know all of you - even your names, even what's going to be said next."

"Try us!" John said.

"Do you know what happened to us?" said Matthew.

"Yes, I do."

"You, Matthew, or should I say: Matthew Jameson? You worked in the city as a stockbroker and, on your journey here, you met people and (to your surprise) have ended up helping them, which is totally out of character. There was the landlord of the pub, who had financial problems, followed by Abigail and her son, Sam, who needed to have a holiday. Then there was the encounter in the woods, which brought you here. You were given a new heart of generosity."

"You, John, or should I say: Big John Jackson? You're a man with a secret (but don't look so worried - it's safe with me). You didn't want the responsibility of running the farm, which your father wanted you to do. Who would have guessed that the adversity of foot and mouth disease would release you - for a much happier life? You were about to take your life in the woods, but along came the light and saved you, bringing you here to find freedom and companionship."

"Newly bold, Esther Thompson! You grew up so shy and withdrawn, but became the boldest of you all. You were abandoned on the steps of an orphanage, and named 'Ruth Harbour'. You grew up without any friends then you also came across the light in the woods. You were given a new name plus an abundance of boldness, and brought here to find friendship."

"Young Jessie Bell. What a journey you have been on! An evening out, meeting your friends in a club, changed your life. You were abducted and abused. Then, as if that wasn't enough, you were attacked in the woods. You were left, frozen behind a tree and too scared to move, until a light came along. In the darkness of your fear, and in answer to your prayers, you were brought here to find comfort."

"Simon Peters: a man of philosophy, with a strong belief in 'fate'. Your life revolved around your childhood sweetheart, Mary, the love of your life. You believed fate brought you together, after losing her for a while. Then she was cruelly taken from you as she lay at the bottom of that cliff. You wondered where fate would take you, not knowing if you would ever find love again. Then you had an encounter with a glowing sphere of light in the woods. You were given hope and brought here to find love."

145

"Hosea Ephraim: A man with Jewish ancestors, who fell in love with a loose woman. Something inside told you to take her for your wife so you married her and she bore you three children. You were happy for a while, then your life was turned upside down. You found out she was going back to her old way of life. The worst part was that she lied about where she had been. She left you but you couldn't let her go and pursued her. In the woods she was confronted with another chance to leave her old life led behind. She declined, thus choosing death - to go the way so many have ended up: forever lost.

"And you, Tom Doulton, the property developer, who had everything money could buy, yet succumbed to the temptation of gambling. You lost not only all your money, but also your wife, children and your home. You met someone surrounded by light in the woods, who knew the emptiness that was inside you and that you were longing to go home to seek their forgiveness. The desire for gambling was taken from you, giving you freedom."

There was silence for a few minutes.
"I knew all this was crazy but after hearing you, Philip, well that has taken it to another level of unbelievable madness!" Simon said.
"I don't know how you did that, but you're good!" remarked Tom.

146

Chapter Nine

Why us?

"Why us?" said Tom, looking at all the others.

"There must be something special about us - or this place. Do you think it's something like the Bermuda Triangle?" Matthew said.

"No! Tell me you don't believe all that; they're just exaggerated stories. We're all normal, rational people, right? Things like this just don't happen to normal people; they only happen in films or books. There's got to be a rational explanation for it," replied Tom.

"Well, you've got to admit something strange is happening around here. We all experienced similar things in those woods. That fog was like nothing I have ever known before. You could feel the evil in it; it was as though it was alive and wanted us. Then the light that came and drove away the fog - it was as if the fog couldn't be there in the light's presence," said Matthew.

"What about that reassuring voice – its owner seemed to know all about us and our needs. And that voice seemed to penetrate right through you, so you didn't want it to stop," added Jessie.

"I know what you mean, Jessie, but how does the tandem fit in? remarked Simon.

And how can I forget what I saw - a sweet child that turned into something from hell," said John.

"As strange as everything else, John. I can't get my head around it."

"Nor can I, Tom. But the 'creature from hell' that John experienced must have been terrifying! I don't know how I would have coped with that," said Esther.

"Me too," said Jessie, "and how weird was it - hearing Philip telling us all about ourselves! It seems to me, we were all at our lowest ebb and looking for a way out.

We each made a choice, and we were given hope and a new life!" continued Jessie.

"It's that hope that has brought us all together," added Esther.

"Not for my wife. She didn't make it here," remarked Hosea.

"Nor Pete, said Tom.

"As hard as it is, Hosea, and it's something that you don't want to hear, but she had a choice and declined the help that was offered to her," said Esther, placing her hand on his shoulder. "It was the same for Pete."

"I think you're right, Esther. We all had a choice," Matthew agreed.

"So – we were all desperate and looking for something to take us out of our misery," summarised Esther. "At least, I know I was."

148

"Yeah, so was I, Esther," said Matthew. "I was looking for an escape from money worries, brought on by my own greed, I might add. Since that encounter with the light, I must confess my worries have gone. I have always led a life of 'looking after number one', but I have come to realise how selfish that was, never giving and always taking. But that person in the light has shown me that there is more joy in giving than there is in receiving," Matthew said.

"For me," Esther said, "I was battling with rejection. The voice not only changed me, but gave me confidence, and it found me more than just a friend." She looked at Simon and smiled, then he spoke up:

"I was a great believer in fate. I just accepted that whatever it gave me was what was meant to be. It gave me love, and cruelly took it away. Having known real love, I couldn't be happy without it, and I found myself wandering in search of love again. My search somehow took me to the place in the woods, excuse the pun: where 'I saw the light'. And you know the rest - I ended up here finding love again," he said, looking at Esther, who flushed with pleasure as all the others turned to look at her.

Tom's voice caused them all to turn to him as he spoke:

"I had success and a loving family, yet threw it all away on selfish enjoyment. But, more importantly, I lost the trust of my wife whom I love. You don't realise what you had until you've lost it. Anyway, all I wanted was forgiveness from my family for ruining their lives. Although they haven't forgiven me, since meeting Gabe (whom I am sure now was an angel or something), I've felt a release of the guilt and regret. And I know now they will forgive me one day," added Tom.

Jessie sat there looking slightly uncomfortable so, knowing that her story might be upsetting for her to talk about, Esther put her arm around her, and said, "Take your time, Jessie."

Jessie braced herself to speak: "If only I had just done what my parents said, I wouldn't be here now. But, no! I had to be rebellious, and wanted more excitement. I only have myself to blame for what's happened to me. I miss my parents and home so much; all I want to do is go home, but I don't know how. I don't even know if they would want me back when they hear what sort of life I've been living. I was looking for a way to go home, when that person in the light came at just the right time to help me in the woods."

"You did well, Jessie," said Esther.

"It wasn't as hurtful to talk about it as I thought. I've just remembered what I was told in the woods: 'I have taken all the pain away'. Tom, do you think Michael – the guy with the posh flat who helped me, was an angel too?" Jessie asked.

"Jessie, I am the biggest doubter. In the past I've heard people telling stories of strangers coming along to help them when they were in desperate situations, and I told them it was just luck. But now, after experiencing it myself (and I don't believe that I'm going to say this), it sounds most probable," replied Tom.

"And you, John?" said Esther.

"With the loneliness and other awful events in my life I came so close to giving up and ending it all. Then, Jerry (whoever he was) brought me here and I've found people that I can call my friends."

150

"Hosea, what do you think brought you here?" Esther asked.

"I suppose that it was the overwhelming desire to hold on to someone that I loved, but whoever that was in the whirlwind of fire, somehow knew that I would be chasing the wind. The reason why I'm here, I have yet to find out," replied Hosea.

All eyes were now on Philip.

"As I told you before, I don't know how I got here. I can only tell you about my life before this happened."

"Oh, please do," prompted Esther.

"Only that I am a writer, and I don't really have much to say about that."

"You must have, Philip. There's something that caused you to be here, otherwise I'm sure you wouldn't be." Esther protested.

"This is all too crazy for me to think about, Esther. Actually, I'm lost for words."

"A writer lost for words? I can't believe that."

"And you believe all the other stuff that's gone on?" replied Philip. Esther didn't reply.

They all looked up as the old, white-bearded man said with a smile: "I think it's time for you all to move on to your new futures."

They had been so engrossed in conversation that they hadn't noticed they were the only ones in the inn, and were surprised to see it was now morning. They had been talking all night, and now none of them knew where they were or where to go. Tom asked the old man, "Is there a town or village near so that we can find transport?"

"There's a town about forty minutes' walk up the track. It was once a small village called 'Ararat'."

John, who had an interest in the history of places, asked: "How far does Ararat date back?"

"No one knows for sure, although some say it's one of the oldest villages around. Apparently people gradually started to move in from afar and, because it has grown so much, it's a town now. At one point the powers-that-be in the town decided to change the name: it's now called 'Modos.' That was its downfall. It's known to be quite dark there - so choose carefully where you stay. Look for the Ark Inn. It's one of the oldest buildings in the town and it's a good, safe place to stay so I recommend you do. One more thing, as you make your way through the woods, don't wander off the track. Stay on it, and you won't get lost. This wood is not a good place to be when it gets dark."

Tom looked at the others, guessing what they were all thinking, as they already knew what could happen in the woods at night. Then there was what the old man said about the town being 'dark', which made him feel wary - *or was he implying that there weren't many streetlights there*? he asked himself.

"The Ark," Tom replied under his breath.

Jessie stood up with her new clothes over her arm and asked the old man,   "Before we go, can I change somewhere?"

"Sure," he said, showing her to a small room.

Just as they made their way to the door, the old man called out, "Remember, you must be out of the woods before it gets dark!"

Outside, they were confronted with morning mist. John was the last to leave and was quite happy trailing along behind the others as they made their way into the woods. A little way up the track, he turned around to see if he could see the inn, but the mist had already thickened and obscured his vision.

As he increased his pace to catch up with the others, he could feel something very uncomfortable inside his shoe and knew he'd have to stop. Seeing Tom up ahead he called and told him.

"Do you want us to wait?"

"No, Tom, you go on. I won't be long - I'll catch you up."

John looked around for somewhere to sit. He could see a tree trunk set back from the track so he made his way to it, sat down and emptied his shoe. When he made his way back to the track to catch up with the others, he found that they were nowhere in sight.

That's impossible! I only stopped for a minute; they've got to be just up ahead, he thought to himself, looking down the track - which was straight for some distance and not yet obscured by mist, although it was beginning to swirl around.

John wasn't the type to panic but he could feel an uneasiness coming upon him, causing him to increase his pace to catch them up. He would feel a little safer with the group, especially after his previous experience. He certainly didn't want to be lost and alone in the woods at night again.

He began to suspect that he must have gone wrong somewhere, but he didn't understand how, as all he had to do was follow the track. Yet he was sure that, if they were on the track, he would have caught them up by now.

As a lad, John knew how to find his way out of any woods. He would take his penknife and cut a nick in a tree trunk or a branch so that he would know that he had been that way already. He decided to follow that principle again, even though the route seemed quite straightforward, and marched on. After some time he found that, although he had been following the track, it had led him back to where he had just come from! Impossible as it seemed, he could have sworn that the woods were deliberately trying to confuse him by changing the layout of the trees and track. He had been going round in circles!

"Tom! Esther! Matthew!" he called out.

The minute he called out, the woods were filled with the sound of crows cawing loudly, making it impossible for him to hear if there was any reply. For a brief moment he thought he could hear a voice, which gave him hope, but the trees seemed to distort the sound and he couldn't tell where it was coming from or even if he'd really heard it.

The others, eventually coming out of the woods, noticed that the mist had gone, which would make it easier for them to find the town.

"At last! That track seemed to go on forever! It's almost as if it didn't want us to get out of the woods."

"My sentiments exactly, Tom," agreed Matthew.

Esther noticed that John wasn't with them and asked if anyone had seen him.

"He was right behind me", answered Tom. "He called out that he was going to stop to get something out of his shoe. I did offer to wait for him, but he said I should go on as he wouldn't be long. I bet he's taken the wrong turn somewhere. I'll go back and find him."

"Oh, I wouldn't, Tom. He can't be far behind, and we don't want two lost. Let's give it five minutes."

"Yeah, maybe you're right, Esther," Tom said. Deep down he didn't really want to go back in there.

John could see an opening up ahead and, even though it seemed to be in the wrong direction, he headed for it, as he knew anywhere out of the woods would be better that in it. He had been concentrating hard on the way he had just come, so as not to get lost again. He glanced back at a tree he had just marked, and, before he knew what was happening, he walked into a bush of brambles, which made him take his eyes off the opening ahead. In the time it took him to release his trousers from the brambles and look up, the opening had vanished!

"This cannot be happening! It was there ahead!" he said out loud. He knew for sure now the wood was playing tricks on him and wasn't going to let him out.

As he gazed ahead, bewildered and helpless, he felt a chill run down his spine. Something made him turn around and, to his horror, standing there was the figure from his nightmares, only he definitely wasn't dreaming. It was the figure of the big guy he had buried! It was just standing there, with its head drooping to one side, and blood oozing from the hole in its chest. Slowly it raised its head and, with its bloodshot eyes boring into John's, rasped in a deep, grating voice: "Killer!"

John stepped back in terror and ran into the woods. As he looked over his shoulder, he could see the figure dragging itself after him, calling: "Killer! Killer!" John was sure he had put some distance between himself and his nightmare, but he realised that, if he thought he was lost before, he was completely lost now and alone. He stopped to listen for the others but there was nothing but silence; there weren't even any bird or animal sounds and he knew that wasn't normal for a wood.

Just as he thought that, the silence was broken by hundreds of crows squawking so loudly that he had to cover his ears.

The noise of the crows made John hurry along the track, giving him no time to stop and think about the direction he was heading. Then, despite the noise, he thought he heard a dog bark. Yes, he did! There to his left, between the trees, he could see a dog looking at him and wagging its tail.

"It can't be! Meg, what are you doing here?"

Seeing his dear old companion warmed his heart and he felt a welcome relief from being lost and alone.

"How did you find me, Meg? Have you been following me? Here, girl!"

The dog just stood there looking.

"Here, Meg! Here!"

"Okay, I'll come to you."

As John made his way over to her, the dog ran off deeper into the woods. "This is no time to play games, Meg!" he called as he gave chase.

John found himself in front of the huge burnt tree again. He noticed this time its branches and trunk were covered in black ivy. It appeared that the tree was in fact the source of the ivy that ran rampant throughout the floor of the woods. As he was looking up to see how far the ivy climbed, he noticed that the unusual black leaves of the tree seemed to have red eyes that were looking down on him. Then he realised they were not leaves but the eyes of hundreds of black crows! A shiver went down his spine. "Meg!" he whispered, so as not to disturb the crows. "Where are you? Come, girl!"

She had vanished. Again he was alone . . . and totally lost; the track wasn't even in sight.

If I keep going straight I must come back on the track somewhere, he thought to himself. Then, from behind him, he heard the words:

"I'm lost."

He turned around to see the transparent, shadowy form of a person. He immediately stepped back and, as he did, the figure walked towards the tree and disappeared into it. Then he heard another voice:

"There must be a way out of here!"

Suddenly the woods seemed to be filled with shadowy figures calling out and wandering, seemingly trying to find their way out. Strangely, John could feel their overwhelming despair at being lost.

He made his way quickly away from there. After a while, he could see a thinning in the trees ahead, which gave him hope that he would find a track there. He was right! With a sigh of relief, he found himself on a track. Whether it was the right one or not didn't matter to him, as any track was better than being lost in the middle of the woods where all sense of direction was gone.

Making his way along the track, he came to a sudden stop. Up ahead was the form of a man in a long, white robe, which radiated light. John stopped and just stared at the figure.

"John," the man said, "All that you have been seeing is only an illusion. Whatever you see or whatever happens, keep your eyes on me, and I will lead you out of here."

John was perplexed, wondering if what he was now seeing was another trick or illusion. But there was something about the man's eyes that was so reassuring that he felt an element of trust towards him. It was the same reassurance as he had experienced with the other two people who had helped him previously.

The man moved off along the track then turned and beckoned John to follow him. John decided to put his faith in him so he obediently followed, keeping his eyes on him.

"John, John!" He heard his name being called from amongst the trees at the side of him. John's natural reaction made him look towards the direction of the voice, and

there, standing in the trees, was his dad. "Dad!" he said, "You can't be here - you died."

"I have come to help you, John. Don't follow him! He's leading you into danger. Come with me; I will show you the way out."

"John, focus on me. Trust in me. I am the way, John." The words brought his attention back to the man in front of him. He remembered what he had said a little while ago:

"All that you see is an illusion. Keep your eyes on me." To help him stay focussed, he kept repeating the words under his breath. *It's an illusion. It's an illusion.*

Step by step, John stayed as close as he could behind the man. Feeling his shoe loosen, he took his eyes off him to look down and see that the lace had come undone. The moment his eyes were off the man, a dense wall of interwoven, twisted and spiked branches surrounded him, separating him from the man. John suddenly stopped.

"Walk through it. It's not real. Trust me, John."

John closed his eyes, put his trust in the man, and walked forward. When he opened them, to his relief, the man was still there.

"Stay close, John."

John didn't need to hear that twice. As far as he was concerned, the man was his way out and nothing in the woods was going to separate them.

It wasn't long before the man stopped. John could see they were at an opening leading out of the woods, which was covered in a shimmering veil of light. It was like a vertical, rippling sheet of water.

"John, on the other side of the veil are your friends. The dark forces in these woods will try with all their might to stop you going through it. All the time you kept your eyes on me, they couldn't hold you. Now, keep your eyes on the veil."

John could see through the veil that his friends were standing there. They could obviously see him, as he could see them shouting at him, but he was unable to hear them. John walked into the veil, but found that there was a force that repelled him backwards.

"Close your eyes, John. Now clear your mind, and think upon only these things: whatever is pure, whatever is true, and whatever is right. Don't be anxious. I will guard your heart and mind with peace. Now focus, John. Have faith, trust me and you will walk through."

Focus! Stay focussed. I've got to stay focussed, he said to himself, stepping towards the veil.

John could feel the force behind him, trying to drag him back. With all his might, he forced his arm forward through the veil, to be grabbed by Tom and Matthew, who were pulling with every bit of strength they could muster. If ever he was in a tug of war, this was it! He knew the stakes were high. It was a battle between good and evil – and the evil did not want to let go of his soul.

159

"Simon, Hosea!" Tom shouted. "We need some help here!"

John could feel the side of his face pressing against the veil. He knew if he could get his head through, the battle was over. From behind him, he felt someone give him the extra push of strength he needed. The next thing he knew, he was lying on top of Tom, Matthew and Simon outside the wood, with the others standing over them laughing.

"There's nothing to laugh about, you lot! We nearly lost him in there!" Tom said, looking up at them from the ground.

"Stop being so serious, Tom. He's out, isn't he?" Esther said.

Getting up from the ground, Tom said, "What on earth was that, John?"

"I don't know, but whatever it was, it didn't want me to get out of there."

"We could see you but we couldn't get through it," Matthew said.

"How come you all got out of the woods?" John asked.

"Apart from taking longer than we thought, we didn't have any trouble or anything like that," replied Tom.

"Then why me? Why pick on me?"

"Don't know, John. What did you do that we didn't?"

"I stopped to get something out of my shoe, that's all."

"Do you remember what he said back in the inn?"

"Who?"

"The old man. He told us to stay on the track and not turn off it. I'm wondering if that's the reason he said it. He knew what would happen."

"Tom's right. I remember him warning us. Did you walk off the track, John?"

"Well, only to find somewhere to sit and take my shoe off. It wasn't far off the track. Come to think about it, that's when I lost you guys, and then again when I was trying to escape the bod . . . uh, I mean when I went after Meg." John had to stop himself for, as terrifying as it was, he knew he couldn't say anything about the figure covered in blood.

"Meg?" said Esther.

"Yeah. I thought I saw my old farm dog, Meg. And again, when I took my eyes off the man, I saw my dead father standing there."

"Man? Your Father! What man?" Tom said.

"He showed me the way out - to the veil, but kept saying, "Don't take your eyes off me.""

"That's it, John. All the time you stayed on the track, you were safe. Thinking back: when we all found ourselves in these woods initially, we all must have wandered from the track."

"You're right, Simon. I know I did. I made a shelter, set well back from the track," exclaimed Tom.

"Yes, I left the track."

"And me."

"I think we all did, if I remember the stories we all told," said Matthew.

"I don't know about you lot, but I have had enough here. I think we'd better get going before something else happens."

"Good idea, John," replied Esther.

"Which way is the town then?" asked John.

"That was the question I was going to ask you, before we realised you weren't with us," said Esther.

While they were all busy discussing which way the town was, they didn't hear a taxi pull up behind them.

The driver, winding down the window, said, "You guys seem to be lost."

"Yes, I think we are. We need to find out which direction to go for the town, Modos," answered Matthew.

"It's left, but it's a long way round by this road. I would give you a lift but there are too many of you. Take the old footpath straight ahead of you, it will take you there."

"What footpath?" Matthew said.

"Cross the road then straight ahead of you, over the stile."

They all rushed over to the other side of the road, leaving Matthew who was watching the taxi drive off. The driver called out the window:

"Have fun!" laughing as he went on his way.

"Did anyone see where he came from?" Matthew asked as he joined the others. "I'm sure we would have heard a car coming in this quiet place. He just seemed to suddenly appear!"

Nobody was listening, as they were all busy looking for the stile in the overgrown hedgerow.

"It's here! Just like he said, Matthew!" John called out.

Tom and Hosea got busy beating the brambles down that had hidden the stile.

"What were you saying, Matthew? You've got that concerned look on your face again."

"I'm not sure, Esther, but that taxi driver appeared from out of nowhere and, on top of that, looked very much like 'James', the taxi driver who gave me a lift from the station."

"What's so strange about that?" asked Esther.

"It's what I saw hanging from his rear view mirror and what he said as he left."

"What was that then?"

162

"'Have fun!' They're the same words he used when he dropped me off before and also it was the same cross on a chain he had swinging from the car mirror."

"It sounds like the same chap."

"Maybe, Esther. Maybe."

Tom, overhearing their conversation, said, "It's probably all a coincidence."

"Thank you, Tom, for your input," Esther said, looking at him.

Matthew was deep in thought about the mysterious taxi driver, but then decided not to waste any more time thinking about the subject.

"Matthew, come on!" Esther called out, as they had all started making their way across the fields.

Matthew soon caught them up. John, who always seemed to be ahead of the others, called out, "Look at that!"

"Look at what?" Tom replied.

"That huge, black cloud up ahead. It looks like a storm's coming!"

It caused them all to stop and look.

"I've never seen such a strange cloud formation, and as black as that, before. We'd better get a move on if we don't want to be caught in it!" said John, quickening his pace and forging on ahead.

"I see what you mean - it's a weird, circular kind of shape," answered Simon.

"I don't know about you, but it looks to me as if it's only over the town," Esther added.

The old footpath soon led them to the town. Sure enough, as the old man had said, at the entrance of the town there was the sign saying: 'Modos.'

"Where now?" Tom asked.

"I assume we just keep on this road. The old man said it's one of the oldest buildings in the town, so we shouldn't miss it," John said.

All the others went on, but John, who had an inquisitive mind, stopped to look at the sign. He had already thought that 'Modos' was a strange name for a town but, as he stood there looking at it, it suddenly dawned on him. If he read it backwards he could see the reason why the old man had said, "Choose carefully where you stay." He remembered reading about the city in the Bible when he was a young lad. Catching the others up, he decided he wouldn't mention it to them, as the day's events had been enough already. It wasn't long before they found the place where the old man had advised them to stay.

Chapter Ten

The Ark

Simon, Hosea and Esther went on in, followed by Jessie. Once again, Phil found he knew what was about to happen and stood several paces back. Matthew and Tom were so busy talking to each other that they hadn't noticed that Jessie had stopped in the doorway, causing Matthew and Tom to walk into her.

"What made you stop like that, Jessie?" Matthew asked.

Before Jessie could answer, Phil said, "She hasn't any money to stay here."

"Is that right, Jessie?" Matthew asked.

"I had all my money taken from me."

"Oh, of course. Don't worry about that, I've got it covered," he said, placing his hands on her shoulders and guiding her in through the door.

165

Phil and Tom followed them inside. At the rear, John glanced up to see the name above the door: *'The Ark'*. *Here we go again*, he said to himself, expecting more weirdness.

As soon as they were all inside there was a mighty crack of thunder and the rain started to fall.

"Looks as if you lot just made it in time!" said the barman.

While the others found a table, John went up to the bar and said, "We were told that you might have some rooms for the night, and that it was a good place to stay."

"Who told you that?"

"The old guy at the inn in the woods."

"What inn in the woods?" asked the barman.

"I didn't get the name, but we were all having a drink there last night. It was a place in the woods on the outskirts of the town."

"I didn't know there was one there, but then I'm new around here. How many rooms then?"

"Seven - if you've got them."

"That's the exact number we have in this place and, you'll be pleased to know, they're all vacant."

As he said that, there was another crack of thunder with the sound of torrential rain falling.

"Sounds as if the heavens have opened," remarked the barman, handing over the keys. After buying sandwiches to take to their rooms, they all agreed to meet at breakfast.

As they sat around the breakfast table, they discussed the strange events of the night before. Because it had affected them so much, it was agreed that they should go back to find the track and the inn. Esther announced that she would have to go back to her room as she couldn't find one of her gloves, which she could have sworn was in her pocket. The others waited until she came down.

Stepping outside, Esther looked up at the sky. "Do you think the rain's going to hold off, or do you think we're going to get soaked looking for the inn?"

"It's going to be fine," said John, brushing past Esther and walking ahead.

Jessie asked Esther if she'd found her glove. "No, but it doesn't matter. They're old anyway and that one had a hole in the thumb. It's just that they were better than nothing."

It wasn't long before they were out of the town and following the footpath across the fields, which would lead them back to the road with the wood opposite.

"I'm sure there was only one opening there yesterday."

"Maybe we didn't notice the other one, with all that was going on, Esther," suggested Jessie.

"So, is it the one on the left or right, John - the track you came out of?" asked Simon.

"I haven't a clue. All I know is that last night when I was trying to get out of there, there was only one."

"And now there are two!" exclaimed Esther.

"I'm just not sure - they both look the same," replied John.

"I say we take the track on the right, and if we don't get our bearings we can always go back and try the other one," suggested Simon.

"Okay, but before we take one step in there, let's keep together and don't take one step off the track," John said, taking charge and leading the way. They all agreed and prepared to follow.

"Can I stay with you, Esther?" Jessie asked.

"Sure, Jessie."

"Good idea, Jessie. You girls stay in the middle of the line. I'll take up the rear," said Tom.

They set off, being careful not to let their feet wander off the track. After a while John came to a halt, stopping at a fork – which presented them with the problem of choosing the one that would lead them to the inn. Tom and Matthew were in agreement: "How can we tell? It was misty, and anyway this track doesn't look overgrown enough."

John raced on ahead of the others further into the woods.

"John we've got to stay together! You know what happened last time you went off on your own!" Esther shouted to him.

"I'll be okay. I'll stay in your sight."

It wasn't long before they heard John shout out: "I think I've found the track!"

They increased their pace to catch up with him.

"There must be a sign with the name somewhere."

"Tracks don't have names, John."

"Esther, don't you remember what he said?"

"Who said, John?"

"The old man at the inn. He said that it used to be a lane and because people stopped using it, it became overgrown and eventually became a track."

"Did he?"

"Yes, Esther! Let's get searching."

"You're so impatient, John."

"The hedges and trees are so overgrown, it could be anywhere," said Hosea.

Matthew, Simon, Esther and Jessie, looked on one side of the track while John, Tom, Hosea and Phil looked the other side.

"Make sure you all keep your feet on the track!"

"How are we supposed to reach to the back of the hedge, John, without stepping off the track?' Esther asked.

John went off along the track and came back with a tree branch.

"Here, try this," he said, giving it to Esther.

Simon took the branch from her and started to beat the overgrown brambles down.

"Look!" said Esther. "I can just see a wooden board and can make out the letter 'S' on it."

Simon continued to beat down the brambles. It wasn't long before they all helped to clear the overgrowth away to reveal an old faded post and a cross rail. They could make out the faded name: 'Salvation Lane'. Immediately the sign was uncovered, the wood was filled with the sound of crows cawing in the trees. They all looked at each other. Jessie moved closer to Esther.

"That's the same name as the station where I got off! Salvation something or other," said Simon.

"You're right!" said Matthew, "Salvation Halt.'

"That's it, 'Salvation Halt', agreed Simon.

"It must have once been the lane that went to the station."

"The inn can't be too far away," Esther said.

Excited, they set off in pursuit of the inn. It wasn't long before they came to a bend. What they saw when they came around it brought them to a standstill.

There, almost covered in overgrowth, was an old rundown building. It was the inn. All of them just stood there in disbelief.

"That cannot be the same place we were in last night. It looks like nobody has been here for years!" John said, following the track that forked off towards the doors, which were just hanging from one hinge.

The rusted hinges creaked as John forced the door open. He stepped back as a large black crow flew out cawing as it made its way up to the treetops.

"Let's go back! We don't know what's in there waiting for us," Jessie said nervously.

John went in, then sticking his head out the door said, "It's fine there's nothing in here."

They all made their way in. The interior also looked as though nobody had been there for a very long time. All the windows were broken and the bar where the old man had stood was now just a pile of rotting timbers on the floor covered with broken glass. Ivy had taken residence over the walls and ceiling of the old building, making it into a haven for wildlife. Esther went over to where she thought they had all been sitting, looking for evidence that it was the spot. All that remained were holes in the thick dusty floor where the floorboards had collapsed with age. They looked at each other, dumbfounded as to how this inn could be so full of life last night and yet was now a dead and abandoned ruin. None of them spoke until finally Tom said:

"This cannot be the same place! There must be another inn nearby. We've gone wrong somewhere along the track."

"No, Tom this is the place. I know it!" replied John.

The others agreed, although they couldn't say why. Then Simon asked Esther what colour her missing glove was. "Like this," she replied holding up the remaining one, which was bright blue and hand-knitted with red stripes around the cuff. Simon removed an item from the debris and dust on the floor, half hidden by a piece of floorboard. He brushed off as much dust as he could to reveal a dirty blue hand-knitted glove with murky red stripes and a hole in the thumb!

"I can't believe it! That is definitely mine!" she gasped. The others were speechless, staring open-mouthed at the glove. "We need to go back to the town to see if anyone knows anything about this place," Esther suggested.

"Yes, but first we need to know if it has a name," John said, leading the others back out through the doors.

Searching through the overgrowth, he noticed what looked like a thin tree covered in ivy but was actually the post of a sign. There, hanging from two old rusty chains was a sign with the faded name of the inn: 'The Saviour's Arms'.

Because the light was fading and there was mist already appearing in the woods, they knew they had to make their way back to the Ark, as they knew only too well the mist was a warning of things that might happen to them, like preventing them from leaving the woods.

Making sure everyone was together, John started off back along the track.

"Don't forget everyone, no matter what you hear or see, stay on the track. I've got a bad feeling that the wood is going to throw what it can at us."

A little way into the woods it started.

The words, "Dad! ... Mum!" from Jessie caused Esther to turn around. Jessie was staring into the woods.

171

"What is it, Jessie? Esther asked.

"Dad and Mum are calling me to them!"

"No, Jessie. There's no one there. They're not real."

"But they are over there. I've got to go to them!"

Matthew put his arms around her, preventing her from leaving the track.

"It's the wood, Jessie. It's feeding on your desires and fears. Stay close to Esther."

"You okay back there, Tom?" called John. There was no reply.

John stopped and looked back to see Tom falling back from the others and looking behind him.

"Tom, I thought we'd lost you there for a moment!"

"I'm still here, John. I thought I could hear something following behind."

"Keep close, Tom."

"Simon, I need you! Please help me!"

Simon let go of Esther's hand and stopped. He turned to the side and, standing there amidst the trees, was his Mary. Her face looked sad and pale.

"Simon, please come to me!" she pleaded, holding out her arms to him.

Although Esther couldn't see or hear anything, she knew there was something trying to lure Simon off the track; in fact he was about to step off into the woods.

Grabbing his arm, she cried out, "Simon! No!"

As if snapping out of a trance, Simon came to his senses. "It's Mary. She needs my help!"

"No, Simon! It's just an illusion of her."

"It was so real, Esther."

"That's what it does Simon. It searches your mind, looking for the hurts and the longings in you and uses them to draw you. That's why no one else can see it or hear it," John said.

"And desires - good or bad," said Hosea, agreeing with John.

Just as he said that, he heard a desperate voice calling out his name. Looking to his left, where it had come from, he saw his wife, Gomer, running and crying out, "Hosea, I'm sorry! Help me!" Shadowy figures of men were chasing her, shouting: "How much, Gomer? How much?"

Realising something was wrong, Tom put his hands on Hosea's shoulders from behind and said, "Keep moving, Hosea. When the evil realises you're not giving in, I'm sure it will give up playing with your mind."

Hosea turned and quickly caught up with the others.

"How much further, Phil?"

"How am I supposed to know, John?"

"If I remember right, Phil, you're the one who knows everything in advance."

"There's a lot to remember, and certain things seem to have to take their course before I can remember them, John."

"Well that was the most unhelpful answer I've ever heard, Phil."

"Let's press on, John. I want to get out of here before anything else happens."

"We're with you there, Jessie!" the others agreed.

Without any warning John stopped, causing Philip to walk into him. John regained his balance without seeming to notice and stood staring into the woods. Up ahead to one side of the track was the figure of a big man. John knew who it was by the gaping hole in his chest and his head that hung to one side. Slowly the figure raised its head, looked at him and rasped, "I'm your secret nightmare!"

"John, what is it?" asked Esther anxiously. John turned around.

"John, your face is white! You look as if you've seen a ghost," she said.

"No, I thought I saw something, but it was nothing. We have to keep moving."

To everyone's relief, they could see bright daylight outside the woods.

"At last! You couldn't pay me enough to go back in there!" Esther announced.

They soon made their way back across the footpath through the field. They could see the sky blackening and rain clouds forming again.

"Do you think we'll make it, Tom?" Esther asked.

"Not sure, Esther," replied Tom in his usual doubting manner but, to their relief, they just made it before the rain started again.

"Find a table while I get some drinks," said Matthew.

"What will it be?" asked the barman.

"Can I just have a jug of squash and eight glasses?" asked Matthew.

As the barman was pouring the squash, Matthew asked him if he knew anything about Salvation Lane and 'The Saviour's Arms.'

"Is that the name of that inn you were telling me about yesterday? Never heard of it but, as I said, I haven't been here that long. I'll tell you what, if you are here tonight, it's worth asking Old Noah."

"Old Noah?" said Matthew.

"Yea. He comes in as regular as clockwork. Apparently he's been around forever. Rumour has it he's as old as the pub, so I reckon he's probably heard of it. You can't miss him - hair and beard as white as snow. He has his usual seat over there," replied the barman.

Matthew told the others.

"Did he say what time 'Old Noah' would be here tonight?' Tom enquired.

"No! But I reckon if we all meet down here about seven, he should be in by then," Matthew replied as they all got up to go to their rooms.

John was the first down and reserved a table. While waiting he observed everyone who came through the door.

"Is he here yet?" said Matthew, arriving next.

"Not yet," replied John.

All the others came down together and sat, hardly saying anything as their attention was on the door, watching for Noah to come in.

John, first as usual, said, "He's here!"

The old man came in and went to his seat, which was at a table not far from theirs. He simply looked towards the barman and, without having to be asked, the barman took over the old man's drink. He stood there chatting with him and pointed over to the group. They were all debating who should go over and ask him about The Saviour's Arms, when the old man, without looking up, took a sip and said, "What do you want to know about it then?"

The entire group, except Philip, quickly got up and took their chairs over to the old man's table. Philip slowly walked over and stood behind them, as he knew what was about to be said by the old man.

"You have questions about The Saviour's Arms, John?"

Here we go again! John thought. He decided that the old guy must have heard one of the others mention his name – how else would he know it?

"We were all out walking in the woods yesterday and we came across an old derelict building. We also found a sign saying: 'Saviours Arms.' It looks as if it had an interesting past."

"Don't forget the lane," Esther said.

"Oh yes, and a lane, or should I say track, called 'Salvation Lane'."

"And the station: 'Salvation Halt," said Simon.

"It looks as though it was quite a busy place some time ago. The barman couldn't help but he thought you might know something about it," said John.

Jessie was staring at the old man's face. She couldn't think where she had seen him before and tried to move her chair closer so she could hear what he was about to say. Smiling, the old man said:

"Do you need help there, Missy?"

"No, I'm okay," she replied but continued trying to get her chair closer.

"Are you sure you don't need my help?"

The minute he said that, it was as though her eyes had been opened. She knew it was the old man she had seen at the station, who spoke those same words to her. She could feel her skin start to tingle. The others moved their chairs so she could get nearer.

"That's a good question! Yes, you are right, John. It was a lovely, peaceful area when this place was a village.

People used to walk or take their horse and carts through the woods on Sunday to the church on the hill, the other side of the woods. They would stop off on their way back for a drink at the inn called 'The Saviour's Arms'. It was a close-knit community; everyone knew everyone and they all helped each other."

"How long ago was that?"

"About three hundred years ago, John."

"What was the church called?" asked John.

"The Saviour's Cross,' Noah replied.

"Is the church still there?"

"No, Jessie. There was a big storm that lasted for three days. The first night the bell tower got struck by lightning and the church burned to the ground. That was the last time the bell rang. The second night the meeting place in the village was hit by lightning and burned down. The last night of the storm the huge oak tree in the centre of the woods was hit by the biggest lightning strike of them all – bursting into flames. All that was left of it was a charred, dead tree that's still there today. After that things started to change."

"In what way?"

"A bad way, Jessie. The morning after the storm, people who walked through the woods noticed that, whereas they would normally hear the birds singing, they could only hear the noise of black crows that had taken over the trees. Others said that the light couldn't get through the tree canopy because of so many crows. All the woodland flowers had died, and in their place were brambles and black ivy spreading throughout the woods and the lane. Word has it, it was like a dark, creeping evil that had come into the area with the storm. It soon spread to the village. As there was no place to discuss

177

things, people were soon arguing amongst themselves, families were breaking up, and love seemed to disappear. Fear soon filled people's hearts and minds about the sinister things that were lurking in the woods."

"What sort of things?" asked John.

"Groups of people had been seen worshiping the big tree in the middle of the night. Some said that they had seen crows pecking at the remains of human sacrifice, which had been buried around the tree, and those who were brave enough to venture in the woods when it was dark would see strange things or hear voices calling them deeper into the wood. They say some of those people never came out. Others found that if they stayed on the lane they were safe."

"What's so special about the lane?"

"You see, John, for decades people have been singing hymns and praying as they were walking along the lane to the church so no darkness can touch that ground.

Then, as time passed, the lane became overgrown but the ivy and brambles, however hard they tried, couldn't completely cover the lane, and so eventually the lane dwindled to a track. It was never really used again, apart from by the occasional wanderer who came across it.

The locals from the old village had many stories to tell about the woods. It was always on a dark, stormy night when those who were 'lost in life' would find themselves drawn into the woods. Most of the time it was when they were at their lowest ebb.

The locals would always know when someone was in trouble. They would hear the church bell sound on the hill, and some say they've seen a light making its way down from the top of the hill into the woods. Many of the strangers who entered the wood were never seen again and, even today, there are stories of people hearing the bell and seeing dark things lurking in the woods.

On quiet, still nights people said that they could hear the cries of lost souls echoing from within the wood, trying to find their way out after wandering off the track."

Tom and Hosea looked at each other.

"They had a choice," the old man said, as if he knew what they were thinking.

Esther squeezed Simon's hand.

"Has the wood got a name?" asked John.

"It's 'Hades Wood'. It was only given that name after the mighty storm," replied Noah.

"Isn't 'Hades' another name for Hell?" asked Jessie.

"Yes, along with a few others."

"It's the right name for that place!" John said, almost under his breath.

"You have something to say about Hades, John?"

"No!"

I wouldn't have thought that, at his age, he would have heard that. He must have his hearing aid turned up full, John was thinking as he took a mouthful of drink.

"I might be old, John, but I don't need a hearing aid."

Not expecting a reply, John almost choked on his drink. *What? Now he can even hear my thoughts! Who is he?*

Noah continued, "There are some who have been in there and have come out to tell their stories, about a light that would appear and rescue them. It was the light of a mysterious stranger. Eventually people called him their 'saviour', and he would come in many different forms. Some said it was a voice, or a pillar or fire. Others said they'd met an angel, but the one that's most common was him riding on a two-seated bike and taking them to The Saviour's Arms inn.

"You said earlier that there were people that never made it out of there. Why didn't the saviour save them?"

"Pride comes before a fall, Matthew. We all have a choice. In their case they were offered help, but they thought they could get out of there in their own strength. As they underestimated the power of the darkness that had taken over the woods, they fell prey to it and are now lost."

Matthew sat there, not sure if he understood what had been said.

"Why on earth use a **bike** to rescue people?" asked John.

"It sounds as if you already know about the bike. Think about it, John. If you had to pick somebody up from a single track in the woods, what form of transport would be more suitable than a two-seated bike, a 'tandem?'"

"Maybe a donkey!" said Tom, grinning.

"As it happens - many years ago, before the bicycle came along, he did use a donkey and then, as time passed, he came riding a tandem. The bike made you question, and now you will remember its significance, Thomas," replied Old Noah.

"Well, I think . . .," began Tom.

"Let him finish," said Esther, nudging Tom in the ribs.

"Ouch! That hurt, Esther!"

Old Noah continued: "Whilst there, at the inn, whatever their problem was would be lifted from them and they would start on a new course in life."

Moving out of reach of Esther's elbow, Tom asked, "I don't suppose there was a barman there?"

"Tom! Let him finish!" Esther repeated, rolling her eyes.

"Why do you ask, Tom?" replied Noah.

"No reason really. The inn sounds so mysterious that I thought there must be an intriguing story to the barman as well."

"As it happens there is a story to tell about him. The innkeeper, a white-bearded old man, would say to any stranger who came in on those dark nights, "Welcome! I have been expecting you." He would call them by their name and put in front of them their favourite drink without them having to ask. Rumour has it his name was Noah too."

"So is every one around here with a white beard called Noah?"

"John!" remarked Esther.

" Well you must admit, Esther!"

Old Noah chuckled and said, "You were made with a great sense of humour! I like that, John. It was quite fashionable, in its day, to have the name 'Noah', John, and you couldn't have a better name for an innkeeper. Tell me, why the interest in the Saviour's Arms and the lane?"

"We came across it yesterday. It looked as if it had an interesting past and, having heard what you've told us, we're right."

"Are you sure that's the reason for asking, John? Don't you all have a story to tell me about yourselves in return? Or a secret, John?" Old Noah replied.

Before the others could answer, John said, "Stories! No! It's as I said, we just love exploring old places."

"If you say so, John. Then there's no more to tell."

Old Noah looked up at Hosea and said. "You're very special, Hosea, don't ever forget it."

They all looked at him.

"What's so special about him?" Simon whispered in Jessie's ear.

"Apparently the Jews are a people chosen by God," she whispered back.

"It appears you have read the Bible. That's good, Jessie," Noah said.

"That's impossible! He heard us whispering," Simon said.

Noah addressed Philip, who was standing behind the others: "You haven't said much, Philip. Is that because you already know all about this story and its ending?"

They all looked at Philip, who was more confused than ever at the realization that there was someone else who knew about his strange ability to know what was about to be said.

Just as they all went to get up and go back to their table, John said, "The name of this town spelt backwards – does it mean anything to you?"

Old Noah smiled and said, "Ah! One of you noticed then. Just as well you listened to the innkeeper's advice about where to stay, otherwise you may not have got here to find out the answers to your questions. I take it you're all staying for the night? If you are, I'm sure that you will have a clearer picture in the morning. I know you will all find what you are looking for in life. Now it's time to move on to your new futures."

And with that he stopped talking and continued his drink. As he didn't seemed to be saying anymore, they all took their chairs and returned to their table.

While they were discussing what they had just heard, Jessie, who couldn't resist another look at the old man, glanced over at his table and was shocked to see he had gone.

"Noah's gone! Did anyone see him go?"

"He must have slipped out without anyone seeing him," replied Tom.

John got up and went outside to see if he could see Noah, but came back in saying: "If he did just leave, he sure got a move on for someone so old. It's a straight road out there and I could see both ways, so I would have seen him if he did go outside."

"Where did he go then?" asked Jessie.

Nobody said anything; they all just looked at each other.

"Why didn't you tell him the real story of what happened to us?" asked Esther.

"What good would it have done?" replied John.

"What did he mean about 'a secret', John? Is it something you haven't told us?"

"Esther, it wouldn't be a secret if I told you, would it? And, anyway, I don't have any secrets."

"Why did he ask you then?"

"He's old and confused, probably getting me mixed up with somebody else."

Esther gave him a look that said, *"You'll keep!"*

"I still say you should have told him the real reasons, especially when he asked: "Are you sure?" There were things that he said that seem very similar to what the old man at the inn said," replied Esther.

Jessie joined in and said, " I couldn't say anything at the table, with him there, but I recognised him as the same old man I saw at the station and then at the inn.

And, by the way he smiled at me, I think he knew that I recognised him."

"Do you really believe that, Jessie?"

"He even had the same name, Simon."

"He did explain that by saying it was a common name. But I give you that, he did look sort of like him with his white hair and beard."

"I'm very sure, Simon! I had goose bumps all over me when he said those same words: 'Do you need help?'"

"Probably the draught."

"Did you say something, Tom?"

"No, Esther," Tom replied, smiling at her.

"I think Jessie is right. I didn't notice it when he said it but, hearing what Jessie said, it's just dawned on me. Just before he left, he said the same words to us as the other Noah said when we left the inn."

"He said lots of things, Esther," Simon said before she could finish.

"As I was saying, Simon, he said: 'It's time for you to move on to your new futures'."

"I didn't hear that."

"You weren't paying attention, Tom."

"Thinking about it, Esther's right, Tom," conceded Simon.

"Don't you think it was weird - him asking us if we had a story to tell? It's as if he knew that we had," continued Simon.

Well, I've had enough excitement for the night. I'm going up to my room."

"I haven't finished with you yet, John. What do you know about the name of this town?"

"Nothing!"

"Then why did you say to Old Noah, does the name of this town spelt backwards mean anything to you?" And why did he reply: "Well at least one of you saw that?" What did he mean by that, John?"

"I forgot to mention it. I suppose, considering what's gone on around here, I should have. Yesterday, when we approached the town sign, you all went on past it, but the name caught my eye. In fact, when the old barman at the inn told us the name of the town, I thought it was a weird name so, when I saw it, I had to stop and look at it. It was then I noticed that, if you spelt it backwards, it's the same name as a town in the Bible: 'Sodom', and that's why he told us to choose carefully where we stayed."

"And I suppose you know the name of this place as well?" Esther asked.

"If you wanted to know you should have looked before you came in. It was right above the door," John said, getting a little bit fed up with Esther questioning him.

With his back to Esther, he got up to make his way upstairs and said, "You can see who's going to wear the trousers between you two."

"What did you say?"

"Nothing, Simon."

"Yes you did, John!"

"I said I must get out of these trousers I'm wearing." John continued to make his way upstairs to his room, leaving Esther and the rest guessing the name of the pub they were staying in.

"Thank you for sticking up for me, Simon."

Putting his arm around her he answered, "You're welcome, Esther."

"He's so grouchy."

"He's had a long day, Esther, and like all of us, he's tired," Tom said in John's defence.

"I'm sure it's called 'The Ark' – don't you remember that's where the old guy told us to stay, but I suppose I'm going to have to go and look," Simon said, making his way outside to see the name above the door. He came back in and said: 'The Ark'."

"This is too much now! First we have 'Old Noah' then we have 'The Ark'. You all must agree with me this is like something out of the Bible," Tom commented wryly.

"Maybe it's because he's been coming here so long and his name is Noah they named the pub, 'The Ark', or maybe he owns it."

"Maybe you're right, Simon," said Esther.

"It's a bit of a coincidence about the town name having the same as one in the Bible though."

"You don't believe in that stuff do you, Matthew?"

"I'm not sure, Tom."

"In the last twenty-four hours I have come to believe a lot of stuff that I wouldn't have believed before."

"Well, I believe it all. I've heard and seen of lots of 'unbelievable' things in the church, and I've read the story of what happened to Sodom and Gomorrah and, if this town is named after it, I suggest we leave as soon as possible."

"I don't know anything about Sodom and Gomorrah, Jessie. What happened?

"You've never read the Bible, Tom?"

"No! I'm not into books."

"It's not just a book, it's a message from God about how to live in joy and happiness and, not only that, it's full of miracles that happened, and a saviour that came to save the lost and broken."

186

"Didn't Old Noah mention a saviour in his story?"

"Yes he did, Tom." I'm sure it's the same saviour in the Bible as the one in Noah's story. All those people in his story were lost or in trouble, just like us."

"I'm still not convinced, Jessie. What did happen to Sodom and Gomorrah?"

"God destroyed both towns because of all the sin and wickedness that was going on in them."

"So you're saying that this place is full of sin and wickedness and God's going to destroy it and, because of that, we should leave?"

"He could do. Anything is possible, Tom."

"Jessie's right, Tom. I have heard about it many times as a boy, from my parents and in the synagogue," Hosea said.

"Even with everything that's gone on, I still have my doubts," replied Tom.

"Well, I don't know about you all. It's been a long day and I'm ready to turn in."

Standing up, Matthew said, "Yea, I've had enough excitement for one day."

Tom agreed.

"I might as well call it a day. I'll come up with you," Hosea said getting up.

"Wait for me - I'll come with too," said Jessie, catching them up.

"See you about nine for breakfast!" Esther called out after them.

"Okay!" came the reply from Jessie.

Esther and Simon were left at the table, holding hands and talking about what the future had in store for them. They were so engrossed in each other that they hadn't noticed Philip sitting at the end of the table, looking lost.

Esther, realising he was still there, said, "Philip, you're so quiet - we forgot about you sitting there! You haven't said much this evening. In fact you haven't said much all day. Are you okay?"

"I'm okay, Esther. It's hard to explain how I'm feeling. It's like nothing feels real to me. Everything I see or hear seems to be a part of my imagination. Maybe a good night's sleep will help me, and maybe I'll wake up in my own bed at home." With that he got up and went upstairs.

"'Night, Philip!" Esther called out.

Phil, convinced he was right about it all being in his mind, still found himself saying, "'Night, you two," even though they might be imaginary.

Simon and Esther's conversation was interrupted by the barman, asking if their glasses were finished with. Looking around they could see that they were the only ones left in the bar. "Yes, they're finished with, thanks," replied Simon.

They made their way upstairs to their rooms and wished each other a good night's sleep.

Chapter Eleven

The Promise

Tom's Promise

As Tom opened the bedside locker drawer to put his wallet and watch in, he noticed a Bible. Although he wasn't into books, he couldn't resist opening it to check out what Jessie had told them about Sodom and Gomorrah. He didn't know where to find that particular account but he started reading the page he had opened. He became so engrossed in the book that he couldn't put it down and soon fell asleep reading it.

He was woken by his name being called.

"Thomas! Thomas! Why, after all that you have experienced and seen, do you still doubt? How much more do I have to make known to you before you believe?"

Tom, still half asleep, thought the voice he heard was a part of his dream. Glancing at his watch, he could see it was 3 o'clock. He closed his eyes and tried to go back to sleep but he was disturbed once again by his name being spoken.

"Thomas! Thomas! Why do you doubt me?"

Tom, realising this was no dream, opened his eyes and sat up in bed.

"Who are you?" Tom managed to say. He couldn't believe he had succumbed to saying that, as he didn't believe in things like voices in the middle of the night.

"I am the one who loves you so much that I gave my life for you."

"Jesus?"

The room began to fill with glowing light and, as if he was watching a film on a large screen, a picture of him and his family in his home appeared. The scene was like it used to be - full of love and happiness, long before the trouble that caused it all to fall apart.

"Thomas, what you can see before you, you can have again. I hold the past, present and future in my hands. Say 'yes' to me. Believe in me and I promise you it will be yours again."

With that the scene faded away, leaving the room in darkness. Tom tried to go back to sleep but was unable to, for all he could think about were the words, "say 'yes'," and the vision of happiness with his loved ones again. The longing in his heart to be back with his family was so overwhelming that when he fell back to sleep he dreamed he was at home with his wife and children, and the break-up was the bad dream.

The morning brought great disappointment when he didn't wake up in his home but in the pub bedroom. The reality of his hopeless situation was brought sharply home to him and he realised nothing would change unless he did. He pondered all that had happened – in the woods, at the inn and in his room. Then, as though scales had dropped from his eyes, he knew without doubt that these supernatural experiences were real. He made the decision to give up on his self-reliance, which he realised had got him nowhere, and felt tremendous relief in putting his trust in the loving saviour who had been trying to help him. He said 'yes' from his heart and immediately felt overwhelming relief and peace flood his being.

He knew inside, with a certainty he couldn't explain, that he had been given another chance with his family and that the desire for gambling was gone. He would be free at last.

John's Promise

Although he went to bed early, John couldn't sleep. Thoughts of what had happened on the farm were plaguing his mind. He had never been a heavy sleeper, for fear of something going wrong with the animals in the night, or a knock on the door by the police or someone saying that one of his animals was out on the road, and that was on top of what took place with the big guy.

His eyes eventually closed and as he was drifting off into a deep sleep, a voice echoed in his mind, "John, come with me, and I will show you your heart's desire and the possibility of it coming true for you. But for that to happen I need to show you the mistakes you've made."

He opened his eyes and there in front of him appeared the same man robed in dazzling white who had set him free in the woods. He was holding out his hand for John to take. Almost without realising, John found his hand reaching out. The minute he took the man's hand, he found himself back at the farm, reliving what had taken place on the night he faced the intruder. He was standing there with the robed man by his side. "I know what you're thinking, John - that you didn't ask for it to happen and you were only defending yourself, which is true. But have you given any thought to where you would have ended up if it was you that had died?"

"I'm not sure if I know what you mean about were I would end up," replied John.

"When you leave this world, what do you think happens to your soul?"

"Never thought about it. I suppose you just go back to star dust."

"Star dust, no. Have you ever heard of Hell?"

"Well yes, but that's just something kids are told by their parents to scare them into being good."

"It's real, John. Unfortunately too many people don't believe it's real and end up there. Like Bernard who didn't get a chance to hear that there was a choice of being with me, or spending eternity in Hell."

"Who's Bernard?" asked John.

"He's the one you buried, John. He didn't know that, when that gun went off, it was too late for him. He didn't get another chance for somebody to tell him about me, although he had heard before and dismissed it. You see, John, nobody knows when it's their time to go."

"You know about that?"

"Yes, John. I knew it would happen, before you knew anything about it."

192

"So you knew my dilemma - about telling the police or keeping it a secret?"

"Yes, John, you always have a choice. Just as you have the choice to reject me or accept my gift."

"What gift? I don't understand."

"The gift of a free pardon for all you've ever done wrong and the promise of eternal life in Heaven with me."

"What's the catch? What do I have to do?

"It's not hard, John. Believe with all your heart and confess with your mouth that I am your Lord. And I will forgive you, fill you with my love and never leave you."

"Even after what I did at the farm?" asked John.

"There is no wrong you can do that's so bad that I won't forgive you, John. It's your choice. Just ask me, and you will have peace."

John found himself getting down on his knees and saying, "Jesus, I believe you and you are my Lord. Thank you for forgiving me."

Instantly he found himself in a field, walking towards a newly painted gate. Slowly turning around, he could see a line of cows behind him, following him towards the gate. He opened it and stepped to one side and all the cows passed through as if they knew where they were going. The cows led John to a milking shed. It felt so natural and he was full of peace as he shut them in.

The scene was disturbed by a voice calling his name: "John! John! Breakfast is ready." He seemed to know where the voice was coming from. Making his way to the house gate, which had a wooden nameplate saying: 'Home Farm,' he could smell the irresistible aroma of bacon in the air, beckoning him in. The gravel path, bordered with coloured, scented flowers led him to the farmhouse door. Turning the large, brass doorknob and opening the door, he beheld a large, pine table around which were seated several farm workers, already tucking into their breakfast.

A smiling, round-faced lady with an apron on, said, "Take a seat, John. One egg or two with your bacon? I must warn you that I've had a complaint that the bacon is a bit salty."

"Two please, Mrs Lott." John thought for a moment: *How did I know what to call her?*

Glancing at her husband, she said, "We were wondering how you are settling in, John?"

"Yes, good! I'm enjoying it - with all the animals, and with the people I'm working with. They're great company."

"We were hoping you would say that!" Mr Lott said, looking at his wife. "You seem to be a natural, and I can tell all the animals like you - even old Lottie there seems to be taken with you, following you about."

"She's like the dog I used to have on my farm."

"You had a farm? That explains why you're such a natural. What happened John?"

John went on to tell them the story of the debts, the disease and losing the farm.

"Well, John, we promise you we're here to look after you now, and you will never have to look back on those times again. If ever you need anything, let us know. You know where to find us."

"Thank you, Mr Lott."

"Eat your food up, John, it's getting cold."

"Will do, Mrs Lott!"

John woke up to the pub room smelling of bacon. Looking at this watch, he realised that he had slept a full nine hours! He couldn't remember a time when he had ever done that. He had slept so soundly, he felt as if his body and mind had been completely renewed and energised.

The smell of bacon in the room took him back to the dream that he had just had. It was so real and vivid that he could recall every part of it: the cows, the name on the gate: 'Home Farm', the owners Mr and Mrs Lott, the smell of the bacon, and Lottie the dog. It had been so wonderful. He had felt wanted and appreciated, surrounded by friendly, caring people and no longer desperately lonely.

Because of the reality of the dream, something inside him told him that this place did exist somewhere. The words: "I will show you your heart's desire" kept replaying over in his mind. A knock on his room door brought him back to the present.

"John! We're all downstairs having breakfast." It was Tom.

"Okay. I'll be down in a minute," replied John. He quickly washed and dressed then made his way down to the breakfast table, where all the others were.

"One egg or two?" It was the pub landlord's wife. Hearing those words again made him think twice before he could answer.

"Err! Two please," he answered cheerfully.

"Sit down, John. I hope you're a little better this morning. Did you sleep well?" Esther enquired.

Tom looked at Matthew as if to say: "Here we go again!"

"I have never slept so well in my life!" replied John, with a huge smile on his face.

Jessie's Promise

After going upstairs with Tom and Matthew, Jessie went to find her room. On the key tag it said: 'Yellow Room'. All the rooms were identified by colour. When she went in it was obvious why it was so called. The walls, curtains, carpet and bedcover were all yellow. To some people that would be too much, but Jessie loved it, as yellow was her favourite colour. It reminded her of her bedroom at home, and the surprise of coming home from a stay at summer camp to find that her father had redecorated the room in her favourite shades of yellow. The thought of that lovely day brought tears to her eyes, as it now seemed so long ago.

Getting into bed, she realised that she hadn't locked the door. She had been so used to not having a lock on her door while she was held in captivity that she forgot. She quickly got up and locked it, then jumped back in and hid herself under the bed covers. It was a habit she had formed to shield her eyes from the overhead light bulb so that she could get to sleep. Again, while in captivity, the light in the room was never turned off. It had been a long day and, with all the walking, it wasn't long before she drifted into sleep.

Jessie found herself standing outside the front door of her home but couldn't go in. As she stood there staring at the door, she felt a gentle hand take hold of hers and a comforting voice said, "I am with you, Jessie, at your side."

Turning, she could see the figure of a man bathed in a radiant light which was so bright that she couldn't see his face. The door seemed to open on its own and she found herself walking through to the doorway of the lounge. She could see her father asleep in his chair with the TV on, and her mother sitting on the sofa with Moses, the family dog, who had planted his chin on her lap. Moses was a present from them on her seventh birthday and she called him 'Moses' as he had long, white fur. She had named him after Moses in the Bible, whom she had always envisioned as having long white hair.

"Mum! Dad! I'm home," she called out.

As if they didn't hear her, they carried on doing what they were doing – Dad snoring and Mum stroking Moses.

"Mum! Dad! It's me, Jessie!" she called out again. Still there was no response. Jessie stood there crying because she couldn't make them hear, then Moses jumped off the sofa and ran towards the doorway, wagging his tail and whining.

"What's up, Moses? What have you heard? There's no one there. Come back up here," her Mum said, patting the seat with her hand.

Jessie reached down to stroke Moses, but found that her hand went through him.

"I don't understand!" she cried. Then it dawned on her that they couldn't see her; she wasn't real!

There was a gentle tug on her hand by the person at her side. In an instant she found herself in her bedroom. It was just as she had left it that night when she told her parents that she was going out to the church youth group meeting. On her dressing table was a vase containing a fresh bunch of yellow flowers that filled the room with their fragrance. On her bed was her favourite old Teddy, 'Mr Ed', which she'd had since she was little. Her mother had taken it out of the storage box and put it there. At the foot of her bed were her neatly folded pyjamas. She could remember Mum repeatedly asking her to fold them up, but it was usually her mother who ended up doing it.

197

Then, as if watching a video, she and her best friend were dancing on the bed to their favourite music during one of her sleepovers. The scene quickly faded and she was back in the yellow room at the Inn. She quickly sat up in bed, wondering if what she had experienced was a dream, but then it had seemed so real to her! It brought tears to her eyes again as she so longed to be at home with her family.

The room started to fill with a misty light, then, the figure that was with her at her home appeared and began to speak.

"Jessie, I showed you the scene at your home so you'd see that the doubts you had about your parents wanting you back were unfounded. Your parents love you so much that they have never given up praying and hoping for your return. Every day your mother has replaced the yellow flowers in your room with fresh ones so that when you came home the room would be welcoming and fragrant."

Feeling more relaxed at hearing the kind voice, Jessie asked, "Why couldn't Mum and Dad see or hear me in the doorway?"

"You were there in spirit, Jessie."

"How?"

"All things are possible for me. I am the way, the truth and the life."

"Will that really happen for me - that I can go home?"

"If you trust in me, Jessie, I promise it will happen for you."

"Are you Jesus?" she asked as a tear rolled down her cheek. "All through my childhood I knew **about** you but I never really knew you. I knew that you came to this world and gave yourself as a sacrifice to pay for our sins. I can't explain why, but it just didn't seem to be relevant to me. I can see now how awful that is - I knew you were mocked and spat upon, I knew about you being whipped with a leaded whip that tore into your back and I knew you were nailed to a cross, and I can't begin to imagine the pain and agony you went through. How could I have thought that was just something in the past that had nothing to do with my life! And why would you be prepared to go through something so terrible?"

"I love you more than you could ever imagine and I don't want to lose anyone."

Jessie remembered a scripture she had learned. "John 3:16: **'For God so loved the world that He gave His only son so that whoever believes in Him shall not perish but have eternal life.'** But they were just words in the Bible – they didn't mean anything to me personally. Now, though, I do want to put my trust in you. I'm sorry for all that I've done wrong and I'm so grateful that you died for me. I understand it more now." As soon as she had said those words, she felt as though someone had poured liquid love over her and she wanted to bathe in it forever.

"Can I ask you about some more things I don't understand?"

"You want to know why you found the Bible so boring and dry. You won't now because it will be full of meaning for you and will tell you more about my love for you and how to live under my protection."

"Another thing that put me off God and all that stuff was the thought of having to obey millions of rules and never having any fun."

"Well, Jessie, you found out where 'having fun' led you." At that she shuddered. "But a life with me is about our relationship, with me loving and caring for you, not about rules."

"What about the ten commandments? Aren't they rules?"

"Yes, you're right. They were rules that no one on earth could ever keep. In fact, they were given to show man how incapable he is of being perfect. That's where I came in. The price was too high and man couldn't possibly pay it so I paid it for him with my life."

"So we don't have to pay anything or obey any rules to have eternal life? That sounds too good to be true."

"No you don't have to pay. But remember you quoted John 3:16: **whoever believes . . .**"

"So – no rules just **believe** in you?"

"Those who believe in me with all their hearts and truly repent from their sins will find that they want to live in a way that pleases me."

"Which is?"

"Love God and love others as much as you love yourself."

"But that's too hard!"

"It's not hard. It's impossible."

"Then how can you expect anyone to do it!"

"It's impossible without **me**. But when anyone chooses to surrender to me, I pour my love into their hearts."

"What if they don't choose you?"

"I never force myself on anyone, Jessie. Everyone is completely free to choose me or reject me."

"I so wish I'd chosen you earlier in my life."

"That's how most people feel when they know the truth about me and experience the joy and freedom it brings."

"I once read that freedom looks a lot like bondage and bondage looks a lot like freedom. I didn't understand it

200

then but now it makes so much sense! All those poor people who are trapped in drug addiction, alcoholism, prostitution, violence – they all thought they were choosing freedom to do what they wanted, but actually they were choosing bondage."

"Yes, like some of the people you've met at the inn."

"I guess that includes me. I thought that going to that nightclub was 'freedom'."

"Now sleep. You have a long journey tomorrow."

She had so many more questions but, unable to resist the heaviness of her eyelids, she fell back to sleep.

She woke up to sunbeams breaking though the gap in the curtains, dancing on her face and filling the room, making it appear full of yellow sunshine. While laying there absorbing the warmth and enjoying the playful show, she noticed there on the pillow next to her was a little white dove feather. Carefully picking it up, she was disturbed by a soft knocking on the door. Instinctively she tensed up, not knowing who would be there.

"Jessie! Jessie! Are you awake? It's me!"

Jessie relaxed and went to unlock the door. She peered from behind it to see Esther waiting patiently.

"Just to let you know that I'm going down for breakfast. Do you want me to wait for you?"

"No, I won't be long. You go on and I'll meet you down there."

Matthew's Promise

Matthew was never one to sleep very much as his mind was always racing - dreaming up ways to make more money, and he was usually at work before the city was awake. But somehow he found he was able to get to sleep quickly.

The office phone rang, disturbing his sleep. It was his friend, Mark.

"At last! I've been weeks trying to get hold of you. How could you do that to me? I thought we were best friends!" Matthew had met Mark some years before at the gym and they had soon become good friends.

"I need that money, Matthew!"

Matthew didn't have a chance to explain as the phone went dead, but it rang again. Thinking it was Mark, he picked up the phone and said, "Mark!"

A voice said, "It's Martha! I trusted you, Matthew! What have you done with my money? That was all I had and I gave it to you to invest so I'd have a little extra to go towards my wedding. You don't know what hardship you've caused me; I had to borrow some cash just to get by. I need that money, Matthew!"

Before he had a chance to speak the line went dead but quickly rang again.

Matthew hesitated before picking up the phone and when he eventually did he heard: "What happened to you, Matthew? You promised to meet with me with my money! I've been looking and asking everywhere for you!"

Matthew recognised the voice. It was an old girlfriend whom he had persuaded to invest her money with him, as she trusted him.

"I need my money, Matthew!"

Again the phone went dead. He sat there looking at it, expecting it to ring again, when the other phone on the desk began to ring. As he went to pick it up the first one rang again. Then the phone on his colleague's desk started to ring, and soon every phone in the office was ringing. The whole room started to fill with voices shouting: "Where's my money?" "I need that money!" With his hands over his ears, Matthew ran out of the office door, to find himself sitting up in bed in a cold sweat with his hands still over his ears. To his relief he realised it had been a dream. The guilt of his past had caught up with him!

Reluctant to go back to sleep for fear of returning to the dream, he got out of bed and stared into the darkness outside the window. In the reflection of the glass he could see the shape of a glowing figure materialising behind him. Turning around slowly he instinctively stepped back, pressing his back hard against the window, unable to say a word.

The figure stood there bathed in dazzling light. Matthew could hear words that were coming into his mind: "Matthew, what you have just seen is the result of the broken dreams of people who trusted you with their money. You need to seek their forgiveness and make amends. You also need to forgive yourself so that you can move forward with your new life."

Matthew formed the words in his mind: *That's what I want to do but I haven't got the courage, or strength to do it.*

"In your weakness I am strong. Trust in me and I promise I will make it happen for you, but you have to give me permission by saying 'yes' to me."

"If you are who I think you are – Jesus, the Son of God, I do actually believe you can do it."

"Then say 'yes' to me Matthew and I will be with you, strengthening you to make it happen for you."

Desperate for forgiveness, Matthew found that the word, "Yes!" came out of his mouth.

"I have seen the sincere remorse in your heart, Matthew, and the generosity that you have shown on this journey."

Matthew had to think for a moment, and then pictures of the pub landlord, followed by Abigail and Sam, her son, entered his mind. He remembered the great feeling he had experienced when he had shown kindness to each of them and he suddenly knew he could do what he had to do.

"Matthew, don't forget that as you take that step, I will be with you - at your side."

With those words, Matthew saw the figure fade away, and the room was once again in darkness. He climbed back into bed feeling as though a great burden had been lifted from him and drifted off into a peaceful sleep.

He was suddenly awoken by the alarm on his mobile. *Some dream that was!* he announced to himself. Then a little thought entered his head, *Or was it?* He made his way downstairs to meet with the others.

Hosea's Promise

The bed looked so inviting that Hosea didn't bother to undress or even get in, he just crashed out on top. As he hadn't slept properly in the last forty-eight hours, he was in a deep sleep the moment his head touched the pillow.

"Hosea! Hosea!" The voice echoed in his mind, making him toss and turn. He murmured out loud: "Gomer . . . Gomer!" A scene filled his mind: he could see his wife standing at the edge of a deep gorge that had a lake of fire running through it. He could see her looking up, crying out to him, "Please help me! I'm sorry! Help me, Hosea!" He saw himself standing on the other side on a higher ledge looking down at her. She was trying to break free from hands in the fire that had hold of her hands, pulling her in. The sight of her in the fire screaming brought him out of his sleep.

He sat on the edge of the bed with his heart pounding and his head cupped in his hands. "Hosea," he heard his name spoken softly. Lifting his head, he saw in front of him the man in the white robe he had met in the woods. He couldn't look directly at him, as the brilliance of the light that surrounded him was too bright for his eyes but he knew in his heart that this was the Lord Jesus.

He heard the man say, "What I have just shown you is the result of Gomer's choice and, because of that choice, where she will be for eternity. You told me that you wanted to find her; now you see why you cannot. She cannot cross over to here and you cannot go there, as there is a great divide between you. I share your pain over her loss. I feel it every time someone rejects me. I offer love and everlasting life, and now I offer it to you. Receive me, and I promise you, Hosea, you will find a true love worthy of the great love that's in your heart. Your children are waiting for you at home."

Hosea found himself stretching and yawning as he awoke from his deep sleep. He could feel the warmth of the sun on his face as it streamed into the room through a gap in the curtains. He sat there for a while pondering his dream, but then a staggering thought occurred to him. Surely it wasn't a dream! The man in white seemed so real, especially with his words, "I promise you will find love again." He knew inside what he had to do to make it come true.

He bowed his head and said from his heart, "Lord Jesus, thank you for all that you have shown me and for your promises. I receive you and I give my life to you."

Joy and peace flooded his whole being and he knew somehow that he had a bright future waiting for him. He couldn't explain this wonderful feeling!

Having refreshed himself he made his way downstairs with a spring in his step.

Philip's Promise

Philip turned off the light and laid down on the bed in the peace and quiet of his room. It gave him a chance to analyse what had taken place in the last forty-eight hours. As hard as he tried, he couldn't figure out how it could be that one minute he was at his desk and, the next, he was staggering, under the influence of drink, in some dark wood. That, in itself, was hard to understand, but to be drawn into a crazy world of make-believe (where you didn't know what was real and what wasn't) was even harder.

All sorts of things were going through his mind. *Maybe all the heavy drinking I've been doing over the last few years has taken its toll on my body and now I'm dead, and this mad place is where you go. Or maybe I'll wake up and it was all a nightmare. Or perhaps I need psychiatric help.*

He could feel himself getting tired and welcomed it, as sleep would give him some relief from the confusion in his mind. He hoped that when he awoke this would be all over and that he would be in his own bed.

He woke to the sound of his wife calling up the stairs. "Phil, you're going to be late. It's 10 o'clock! The agent will be here in an hour to pick you up!"

Phil deliberately kept his eyes shut. Although the reassurance of his wife's voice told him that he was back at his house, he was still unsure of what he would see when he opened them. Would he still be in the make-believe world or would he be in his bedroom at home?

Slowly opening one eye, he saw, to his relief, that he was at home.

That's it! I'm finished with drinking! That was some dream! he said to himself.

It wasn't long before he was on his way, with his agent, to the store for the book signing. As they pulled up outside, he could see that a long queue had formed already, all waiting to buy his book and have them signed. Success had been a long time coming for him, as the sad event of losing a dearly loved child had made him stop writing for a long period. But now he was back, seeing his dream being fulfilled as a successful writer.

Sitting there signing a book, his eyes started going misty. Everyone in the room seemed to fade from colour to grey and then became transparent. He could feel something was wrong and started to rub his eyes. As he did, he felt himself being transported away from the store into a dark place. He was back in the pub room, lying on the bed. For a brief moment he thought that he was really at home. But now he was more confused than ever, not knowing what it was that had just happened.

He looked at his watch and noticed he had been asleep for twelve hours. But, in stunned disbelief, he saw the hands of the watch start to go backwards, stopping at 10.05! The watch had reset itself to the time he went to bed!

Recalling his short dream, he realised that it was the only time since being trapped in this new world that he didn't know beforehand what was going to happen. However, a strange feeling told him that something new was about to take place in the room.

His expectancy was justified as, lying on the bed gazing up at the ceiling, he saw a small dot of light appear. The dot seemed to grow and get brighter and the more it grew, the brighter it got until the whole ceiling was lit up.

Then, from out of the light, a voice said, "Philip, all that has happened to you, I made happen. The things you have seen and heard are a part of my plan for you to have success, but it has been the alcohol that has stopped it. Before you were born I planned for you to be a successful writer, and you will be, if you believe and trust the things I say. And now I want you to write a book for me. You have met the characters and their stories have been unfolding. I heard you say, "How did I know that was going to happen?" and "How did I know what that person was about to say?" It was all part of my plan for you to write the book." Every word that was spoken caused a wave of light to bounce across the room.

The voice continued to speak: "The encounter in the woods was real, Philip. The alcohol had a strong hold on you, but I have come to break it off you for good. I am the way, the truth and the life. I promise you, when you believe in me and the truth of what has happened to you, it will set you free."

With those last words the light on the ceiling faded back into a small dot then disappeared.

Phil just laid there, not able to take his eyes from the ceiling. Lingering in his mind were those six words: *The truth will set you free. The truth will set you free. The truth will set you free.* The rhythm of the words caused him to fall back to sleep.

Woken by the light from the window, Phil didn't want to open his eyes as, again, he was unsure of where he would be or what he would see. Slowly squinting from under his eyelids, he could see he was in the pub bedroom, not (as he had hoped) in his home. He tried to recall what had taken place, then he could hear in his head: *The truth will set you free. The truth will set you free.* Phil found himself repeating it with his lips. The instant he spoke those words everything became clear to him and he knew what was real and he knew in his heart who had said it. "I believe you and I trust in you for my future, Jesus!" he said aloud. He felt great peace in his heart and he knew he'd never want alcohol again. He didn't know how he knew, he just **knew**!

He also knew he had to stay where he was a little longer if he was to fulfil his dream of being a successful writer and that, if he trusted in the words the Lord Jesus had spoken, all would be okay. With a look of relief on his face, he went downstairs.

Simon's Promise

Simon quickly got into bed and drifted off to sleep thinking about Esther. Esther was laughing as she ran across the flowered meadow, trying not to let him catch her. He had often chased her as it was a game that gave them so much fun. He quickly caught her and they tumbled to the ground. As she turned over to face him, Simon saw a face that he was not expecting to see. It was the face of Mary!

The scene quickly faded as she said: "Let go, Simon!"

Immediately another scene appeared. Simon found himself on the front of a two-seated bike and heard laughter from behind him, followed by the words: "You're not pedalling fast enough! Faster, Simon! Faster!"

In front of him was the crest of a steep hill they were trying to ascend.

"It's not me who's not pedalling fast enough, it's you Esther!"

He expected a cheeky reply but there was only silence so he stopped the bike and turned around to see why. He saw only the fading image of Mary's face saying, "Let go, Simon!"

He then found himself sitting on the cliff edge, holding hands with Esther as they watched the sun going down below the horizon. It had been a beautiful day up to that point. He got to his feet and took Esther's hand to help her up. He had a strange feeling that he had been here before, knowing what was about to happen, but unable to do anything about it. He was suddenly looking down at Esther, holding onto him with one hand as she dangled over the cliff. As she looked up at him, he could see that it was the face of Mary again, and she was saying: "Let go, Simon! Let go!"

Waking up with his heart pounding, he could sense someone standing at the side of his bed. He turned his head to see the glowing outline of a man.

With his heart still pounding, he heard the words, "Simon, what you have just seen shows that you are harbouring guilt because you feel that you have betrayed Mary's love for you. That guilt is hindering you from leaving your past behind and embracing your new love, Esther, yet Mary would have wanted you to move on and be happy. It's time to let go."

When the voice stopped speaking, Simon could hear church bells, filling the room with their sound. He could see himself standing at the front of the church with a friend at his side. The oak doors behind made a creaking noise as they were being opened and he could hear the sound of people shuffling in their seats as they turned to look. Simon turned around too and saw a beautiful woman dressed in a flowing white dress with a coronet of colourful flowers in her hair. It was Esther - walking down the aisle towards him. Hand in hand, they faced each other to say their vows. He could hear himself saying, "I do."

The scene faded once more, for him to hear: "Simon you have always put your trust in 'fate'. All that you have just seen I promise you will happen for you, if you now put your trust in me. I am the giver of love to all who seek me for it."

Simon closed his eyes. He knew, without being told, that this glorious person was Jesus. He longed to have the wonderful future he'd been shown and it was a tremendous relief to him when he uttered the words:

211

"Yes, I believe and trust in you. I want you to turn my life around."

Simon rubbed his eyes as he opened them to see the room was dark once more. He lay there, wondering if it had all been a dream, but as he became fully awake, he could feel that a weight of sorrow deep inside him had left, and had been replaced with a love that he almost couldn't contain.

The morning came and, despite not having had much sleep, he felt refreshed and eagerly hurried downstairs to see his lovely Esther.

Esther's Promise

Esther didn't feel sleepy at all. In fact, as she snuggled under the bed covers, she felt that she could dance all night – such was the joy of finding love after all the years of loneliness. However, she did eventually fall asleep and was dreaming about Simon and her newfound friends, when somebody started pulling the covers off her and shaking her shoulder to wake her.

"Ruth! Why aren't you up with the others and your bed made?"

It was a member of staff who had been sent to find out why she was not at the breakfast table with the other children. She was made to get dressed quickly, make her bed, and was then escorted to breakfast. The other children, when no staff member was looking, made fun of her at the table and the pain of loneliness returned, confirming to her that her newfound friends were only a dream, brought on by an overwhelming longing.

Throughout the day Ruth reminisced over the dream to cheer her up and to alleviate the aching loneliness. The time for bed eventually came around and, as she lay there once again, she prayed that God would give her the same dream - where she had so many friends and was loved, even if it was only for a little while.

She woke up to find she was a young woman sitting in a dark wood amongst fallen trees and undergrowth.

"Ruth! Ruth! It's your old friends. We've missed you!" called voices from out of the darkness.

She spoke back to the voices, "No I didn't ask for you; you're not my friends. Go away!"

"We are your only friends, Ruth - Loneliness and Depression. You have no others."

"You're not my friends! I have new friends."

"They're only a dream! They're not real - we are. We're the only friends you will ever have, Ruth."

With her hands over her ears, she cried out, "My name is Esther!" The moment she said those words she found herself back in her room at the inn and soon a new scene unfolded. She was standing in front of a door, which was outlined with a brilliant light that was forcing its way through the thin gaps around it. The door slowly opened and Esther entered a room, which was filled with bright light.

Although she couldn't see anyone, she heard a voice saying: "You are wondering why you have experienced those hurtful memories, and why your new friends don't seem real. I promise you, Esther, those lonely days are over – they are just memories. If you put your trust in me, Jesus, I will give you a life full of love and many friends. If you will say 'yes' to me, I will always be your friend and you mine."

Overwhelmed with joy and hope at those words, Esther breathed, "Yes, oh yes, I will put my trust in you, Lord Jesus!"

"Whenever you need me, you can call me and I will be there. You will know my voice. I have one more vision to show you of things to come:"

The sky was blue and birds were singing as she saw herself walking up a gravel path to the doors of a church. Esther soon found she was at the altar, standing by the side of a man and, as she turned to see his face, she saw it was Simon. After the ceremony they made their way out of the church, and then surrounding them were all their friends, showering them with confetti. She felt as though her heart would burst with joy.

Esther awoke to the sound of birds singing outside her window. Drawing the curtains, she could see that it was a beautiful day. The atmosphere in the room seemed to be filled with a loving presence, making her believe that what she had experienced last night was very real. She lay on her bed soaking up the wonderful feeling and, not wanting it to end. She hadn't noticed what the time was. She remembered that they were all meeting downstairs at nine but it was only the thought of seeing Simon that made her come out of her reverie to quickly get ready.

Passing Jessie's door, she knocked and called, "Jessie! Jessie! Are you awake?" It's me Esther. I'm just going down for breakfast. Do you want me to wait for you?" Jessie told her to go on.

Hurrying down, she saw the face of Simon smiling at her and offering her his hand at the foot of the stairs.

Chapter Twelve

Going Home

When they had finished breakfast, John leaned back in his chair and said, "What now for us all?"

"Not sure, John. It certainly has been a strange few days."

"You can say that again, Tom!" Matthew added.

"Well, after last night, I know what I have to do. I'm going to go home to my family and make things right with them."

"What happened to you last night then, Tom?"

"You don't want to know! All I'll say is that I was always a doubter, but I'm now a believer - in stuff that I never would have thought possible."

"It sounds very much like the night I had," remarked Matthew, getting up from his chair to leave the table.

"You can't say that, Matthew, and then leave!"

"I would say that you wouldn't believe me but, after the last few days, I think you would, Esther."

"So?"

"So what?"

"What happened?" Esther urged.

"I had a visitor in my room."

"What visitor?"

"Not **just** a visitor, Esther."

"I don't suppose it was a figure, so bright you couldn't see him properly?"

"As it happens, Jessie, it was."

"He came into my room too." Jessie replied.

"Mine too," said Simon.

"And mine," added Hosea.

"The visitor, Matthew, what happened?"

"It started with a vivid dream; I was shown my past and where it had all gone wrong. The visitor told me what I had to do to make things right and I was shown a glimpse of things to come for me."

"Was it a good future, Matthew?"

"Yes, Esther, a good one! I have been given the opportunity to start again, but before I can there's something that I have to do. A lot of people trusted me with their money, but I betrayed them. I know I have to go back and put things right with them before I can go forward. Then I'm going to turn my knowledge of making money to help those who haven't got much and also there's a certain little person I promised that I would go back to see."

"We're pleased for you, Matthew," the others all agreed.

"Thanks!" Matthew said.

"Hosea," Esther said, inviting him to speak.

"I was so tired that, when I saw that bed, I just crashed. I thought it was just a nightmare, but I had an awful vision of my wife calling me to help her. She was being pulled into some sort of fiery lake and it was so horrific that it brought me out of my sleep. I'm glad it did as I couldn't stand the sight any more."

"That sounds horrible! What happened when you woke up? I assume there's more," said Esther.

"Yes, there's more, Esther. I was on the edge of the bed when I heard my name being said and, when I looked up, he was there."

"He?" Esther said.

"The same man who was in the woods. He said a lot of things that, at the time, sounded like nonsense to me. Then last night, after what he showed me, it all became clear and, as upsetting as it was, it seemed to make sense. I have been chasing the wind, but now I'm going home to my children."

"Come on, Simon, tell us about your visitor," Esther said, turning to Simon.

"You're so impatient, Esther," Simon remarked to her. "Well, I too was dreaming. In fact I had three different ones that seemed to blend into one another. In each dream I seemed to be with you, Esther, but each time your face changed to Mary's and she kept telling me to let go.

The third one brought back the tragedy at the cliff top when I lost Mary. I was showing you, Esther, the sunset and then suddenly you were hanging over the cliff, and I had you by the hand. You looked up at me, but it wasn't you - it was Mary, saying: "Let go, Simon! Let go!" It was so real that it brought me out of my sleep and I was just sitting up, covered in sweat, when I saw a dazzling figure standing at the side of my bed.

He told me that he was showing me those scenes from my past to release me from the guilt that I felt over betraying Mary. I know now that I am free of it and ready to move on with my new life."

Esther squeezed his hand.

"I read an article once about the meaning of dreams. Although I didn't believe it when I read it, it seems obvious that you've been shown a message by it."

"I guess you're right, Tom," said Simon. "I haven't finished yet. The next part wasn't a dream - more of a vision. I know that because I was wide awake. I could hear church bells, and then I saw us getting married, Esther. The figure told me that the vision that I had just seen was what was waiting for me, and the next thing I knew it was morning." Esther flung her arms around him.

"By the sound of it we all seem to have another story to tell, or should I say dream? Come on, Esther, your turn - tell all," said Matthew.

"I was having such a lovely dream about you all when I was woken by someone pulling the bed covers off me and suddenly I was a child back at the orphanage. It was so strange - it was as if I was an invisible stranger in the corner of the room looking at myself as a little girl, so lonely and sad. It brought back awful memories of that place, which I thought I had forgotten. I took my eyes off the little girl for a moment and, when I turned back to see her, I was a grown woman sitting alone in the woods. Voices were calling to me, trying to convince me that I was still Ruth who didn't have any friends and that none of you were real. I can't explain it but something made me shout: "My name is Esther!" then I found myself in my room upstairs. As I walked through a door into a room filled with light, I could feel the effects of this light washing every hurtful memory away and a voice in the room revealed to me the meaning of the dream. It was that my past couldn't hurt or hold me any longer. It felt like the person in that room was a really close friend that I could always rely on to be there for me. Then I found out he was."

Turning towards Simon, she said, "Then, like you, Simon, I saw a beautiful day and we were getting married. The dream ended with us standing outside the church, being showered with confetti - thrown by our many friends, who were surrounding us. Then I woke up and, although a little disappointed it was only a dream, I knew that the dream was to show me that it could come true." With those words, she leaned towards Simon and kissed him.

"I suppose, if I want to leave here, I'd better get on with what happened to me."

'Yes please, John!" came an excited little voice from Jessie.

"Having laid there for some time, I must have drifted off to sleep. Then I heard a voice saying, "I'm going to show you your heart's desire," and a man in a robe appeared holding his hand out for me to take. Dreams are so weird!"

"They sure are," said Matthew.

"It's like nothing makes sense, and anything can happen without any explanation."   Already John had decided not to say anything about the first part of the dream as it would have meant telling them about burying the intruder, and that was to stay between him and the Lord. He started by saying: "One minute I was in my room, then I found that I was walking in a field with cows following me. After that I joined the farmer's family and farmhands for a wonderful, cosy breakfast. There was even an old dog sitting there at my side, waiting for the scraps from my plate."

"Sounds like you were at home, John."

"That's exactly what I was thinking in the dream, Simon, except that at my old place I always had breakfast on my own. The feeling I had at the table in the dream was something I've always desired - to be surrounded by a real family in a homely atmosphere. The disappointing bit of the dream was that I never did get to taste the eggs and bacon. I woke up in my room."

"Well, at least you've had some real eggs and bacon now," laughed Tom.

Every one could see that Jessie was eager to tell about her experience, which led Esther to say, "Go ahead, Jessie. Tell us what happened to you."

"I dreamt that I went home; well I think I dreamt it but it seemed so real. I was standing in the doorway but couldn't go in. At my side appeared a figure encased in light that took my hand. We went in and I saw that my parents had never given up on me. They had put fresh flowers in my room and kept it ready for me.

I remember crying with longing to be home, and the figure told me he had shown me this because I thought they wouldn't want me back. Now I can't wait to go home."

Esther gave her a hug and said, "Ring them, Jessie, as soon as you can."

"Yes, I will. But, you know, the best thing to come out of all this is that the 'stranger' isn't a stranger any more. He's someone I've heard about all my life but now he's real to me. He's loving and kind and wonderful – and I never want to go back to my old life, without Him."

"So, did he tell you his name, Jessie?" asked Esther.

"He didn't have to! He's my beautiful saviour, Jesus."

The others all had knowing smiles. They all knew who he was, this gentle, loving 'stranger' whom each one had already put their trust in.

"Come on, Phil, what happened to you?"

"What makes you think something happened, Esther?"

"We've all had something happen to us, so I'm guessing something must have happened to you, didn't it?"

"I'll tell you later," he said, reluctant to say anything until he understood more himself about this book he was supposed to be writing.

Jessie, who was impatient to go home, left the table to see what the weather was like outside. As she opened the door, there in front of her in the sky was a magical scene! It was a huge rainbow but, more exciting for her was that, as she stood there, the colours of the rainbow were shimmering all around her.

"It's the rainbows end!" she breathed, like a little girl full of wonder. She ran back through the doors, calling to the others: "Come and see! It's beautiful!!" then ran back outside.

They all got up and hurried outside to see why Jessie was so excited. Each one stood there looking up at the rainbow with its seven vivid colours, each blending into the next, like watercolours on wet paper. Jessie was like a child dancing in the rays of the rainbow, which were changing colour as she danced round and round.

"I've always wanted to see the place where the rainbow ended!" she said as she continued dancing.

Humouring her, Tom said, "Oh yes, Jessie. Did you find the pot of gold?"

"Tom, look where you're standing! Look at the colour of your shoes! They look gold!" Simon said, pointing down at his feet.

As Tom looked down, in his head he heard the words: "All things are possible."

Jessie stopped dancing and, looking up, said, "It's God's promise."

The moment she said that, they all remembered the words that were said to them in their dreams: "I promise you it will happen."

"Come on, Jessie, we'd better go back in and get ready if we are going," Phil said, knowing that the sooner they said their goodbyes the sooner he would be able to go home and start a new life and a new adventure.

Led by John, they all made their way back in. John went to the bar. He had noticed that there was someone new behind it. "I don't suppose you've heard of a 'Home Farm' around here?"

"Home Farm. Is that old Abel Lot's place?"

"I know the names are Mr and Mrs Lot, so it sounds like it's the place."

"Well, if it is, turn right out of here, and keep going straight till you are out of town. You should come to an old stone bridge. Once over the bridge, fork right. There should be a sign saying: 'Jordon Lane'. It's somewhere up there."

"I think I've got it, thanks." John sat down with the others, who were discussing where they were all going.

"I could see you talking to the barman. What are you up to now, John?" Esther enquired.

"I was just asking if he knew where Home Farm was."

"Home Farm?"

"It's the place I saw in my dream. As I'm so sure it exists somewhere out there, I decided to check it out with the barman - who confirmed my hunch by telling me that he has heard of it."

"Is it far?"

"Amazingly no, Esther, it's just outside of town."

"I take it then, you are going to stick around here, John?"

"I guess so, Esther. I've got nowhere else to go, and if this Home Farm is anything like the Home Farm in my dream, then that's where I'm going. I take it that you and Simon have already discussed where you're going together?"

"What makes you think we're together?"

"It's pretty obvious, Esther."

"I was joking, John. Of course we are," she said, looking at Simon.

"We'd better be!" remarked Simon.

"All I know is we had the same endings to our dreams - a promise of love and a vision of our wedding. And so it doesn't matter where we end up, but we do know that we will spend the rest of our lives together." Simon nodded and kissed her on the cheek for saying that.

Matthew tapped his glass and got everyone's attention. "Well I suppose this is where we all say our goodbyes. It seems that bringing us all together was part of a divine plan. We came together as strangers, but we're parting as friends. To stay in touch with one another, what about if I give you all my number?" They all agreed and swapped details.

"I'm going to ring for a taxi to take me to the station. Anyone else want a lift there?" Matthew announced.

Tom and Hosea both answered: "Yes" at the same time.

"Can I come with you?"

"Of course you can, Jessie," said Tom.

"Where are you going?" asked Hosea.

"The station, if that's alright?"

"Do you think I could be dropped off afterwards? I left my car in a village not far from here."

"I'm sure that's alright. I'll just mention it to the driver when we get in," replied Matthew.

Matthew went over and asked the barman if he could ring for a taxi.

"Well this is it. I guess we'll be seeing each other again this time next year," Matthew said, as they hugged each other.

The four made their way outside to wait for the taxi. No sooner had they stepped outside, the taxi pulled up. Tom, Hosea and Jessie got in the back and Matthew sat in the front next to the driver.

"What've you got there, Jessie?" Tom said, noticing that she was looking at something in her hand.

"Oh, it's only a little reminder," she said, closing her hand around the little feather.

"Station is it, Matthew?" the driver said with a smile.

Matthew had been busy doing up his seatbelt but something about the voice and the mention of his name made him glance quickly at the driver - to see that it was James, whom he'd had the mysterious encounter with before. Smiling back at him, he said, "Station, James!"

"Well, I'll say my goodbyes to you three. I'd better get off, if I'm to find Home Farm before it gets dark. We all

224

know what can happen to you around here when it get's dark!"

"That's true, John. I hope it's the place you're looking for," said Esther, getting up and giving him a hug.

"Me too, John," Simon said, also hugging him.

"And me, John," added Phil.

As John made his way out, Esther called out, "What was that secret of yours, John?"

John merely turned and smiled as he went through the door.

"Well, Phil, that just leaves you. You thought you were going to get away with not telling me what happened to you last night."

"Still bossy, Esther, aren't you?"

Philip was about to take a mouthful of water before he began to tell them, when Esther, while turning to look at Simon, accidentally jolted his arm - making him spill his drink all over the table.

"Sorry, Phil, that wouldn't have happened if you'd got on and told us when I asked you earlier."

Phil was busy trying to mop up the water, when Esther rested her hand on his shoulder and said, "What did happen last night, Phil?"

Phil didn't answer, but felt someone shaking his shoulder. He could hear: "Phil, Phil, Philip! Wake up! Have you been there all night writing?"

With an empty wine glass in his hand, Philip raised his head from the desk, where the contents had obviously been spilt. With a look of bewilderment, he said, "I'll tell you in a minute, Esther."

A stern voice said, "Who's Esther?

Realising that it was his wife, he said, "I must have dropped off without realising."

"I wish you wouldn't drink so much, then this wouldn't happen," his wife said, mopping up the wine. "And you can tell me about Esther later".

"I can assure you it won't happen again. I have finished with drinking," replied Philip.

"If you say so, Philip. What makes you so sure this time is any different than the other times?"

Philip looked at his wife and said, "Believe me, I have quit. I have no desire for it anymore."

His wife had never heard him speak with such assurance in his voice and knew that something must have happened to him overnight for him to speak like that. Changing the subject, she said: "How far have you got with the book?"

"Oh, I'm scrapping the spy story now and starting something completely different," Philip replied. "This time it's going to be based on truth, and I've met all the people who will be the characters."

"So, will it have a happy ending?"

"Oh, yes! I know now why I've been given this book to write. People don't realise that there really is a supernatural realm and that evil powers delight in entrapping us into bondage of one kind or another. They also don't know that there is a far superior power that wants to set them free!"

*   *   *   *   *   *

Tom Doulton made his way to the bar with a look of confusion on his face. The white-bearded old man behind the bar smiled and said, "Usual, Thomas?"

'I am the light of the world. Whoever finds me will never walk
in darkness but will have the light of life.'
John 8 v.12